P9-CDA-318

Freeport Public Library

314 W. Stephenson
Freeport, IL 61032
815-233-3000

Each borrower is held responsible for all materials charged on his
card and for all fines accruing on the same.

VIKING
Published by the Penguin Group
Penguin Putnam Inc., 375 Hudson Street, New York, New York 10014, U.S.A
Penguin Books Ltd, Registered Offices: Harmondsworth, Middlesex, England

First published in 1998 by Viking, a member of Penguin Putnam, Inc.

1 3 5 7 9 10 8 6 4 2

LIBRARY OF CONGRESS CATALOGING-IN-PUBLICATION DATA
Dirty laundry : stories about family secrets / edited by Lisa Rowe
Fraustino.
p. cm.
Contents: Aunt Gladys / B. Coville — About Russell / R. Williams-
Garcia — Words / D. C. Regan — Stage fright / A. G. Hines — Rice
pudding days / S. C. Bartoletti — Waiting for Sebastian / R. Peck —
I will not think of Maine / M. E. Kerr — FRESh PAINt / L. R.
Fraustino — Passport / L. H. Anderson — Something like love /
G. Salisbury — Popeye the sailor / C. Crutcher.
Summary: A collection of eleven short stories by various authors
dealing with situations which a family or family member tries to
keep secret because of an underlying problem.
ISBN 0-670-87911-8 (hardcover)
I. Problem families—Juvenile fiction.   2. Children's secrets—
Juvenile fiction.   3. Children's stories, American.   [1. Family
problems—Fiction.   2. Secrets—Fiction.   3. Short stories.]
I. Fraustino, Lisa Rowe.
PZ5.D635   1998   [Fic]—dc21   97-52309   CIP   AC

Printed in U.S.A.
Set in Gill Sans

DIRTY LAUNDRY

STORIES ABOUT FAMILY SECRETS

Edited by Lisa Rowe Fraustino

VIKING

Introduction

I owe this anthology to a box of paper clips.

My conscious fascination with family secrets began the year paper-clip necklaces were the rage. You'd string regular paper clips into a chain, then cover each clip with colorful contact paper. My year-younger sister, the pretty one, therefore the popular one, managed to find a benefactor in the cool group and got herself a chain early in the craze. I, however, did not have the proper connections, and my parents refused to waste their meager resources on paper clips and contact paper. Without a string of paper clips around my neck, I was marked as an outcast for all to see.

I was a trustworthy child. Teachers often sent me to the office with their messages or the attendance list, accentuating my outcast status. The secretary knew me by name. She smiled when she saw me and asked me how I was. Perhaps she would even have given me a box of paper clips had I dared ask. But I didn't. I just eyed them enviously every day, huge neat stacks of them in the supply cabinet between the index cards and pencils, tempting me. Oh, why couldn't the secretary have kept that closet door closed?

One day she wasn't at her desk. The principal wasn't in the next room. The office was empty. Empty of people, but not of paper clips. The pile beckoned, a pile of more paper clips than all the teachers in my little school in rural Maine would ever, ever need. Who would miss one itty-bitty box of paper clips? Nobody. My heart palpitating, I reached for the box and crammed it into my pocket. I swear it burned my leg.

My sister had contact paper left over from her necklace. I asked for some. "Why do you want that?" she sneered. "You're just copying me. Besides, you don't have any paper clips."

I did so. But how could I tell her that? She knew I had no money to buy them. And I'd sooner tell the truth than lie. The solution was clear. I would hide the paper clips under the sink, far in the back, where nobody would find them, until I could figure out what to do.

As the days ticked by, my secret changed me. Every time I went into the office, I couldn't look the secretary in the eye—if I did, I was sure she'd see what I had done—and I kept my back to the supply closet. Even if nobody else ever found out that I was not the honest, trustworthy girl they thought me to be, I knew. I knew it well, and I carried my guilt in my stomach, where it grew rusty and pitted, just as the unused paper clips did under the drippy sink pipes. And to this day, those rusty paper clips pinch me in the stomach to tell me when something is wrong.

Part of finding the answers in life is having the right questions. If I had a secret, I, the perfect oldest daughter, the honest one, the smart one, what did that suggest about everyone else? What embarrassing or painful or shameful acts were rusting out under the dripping con-sciences of family and friends and teachers and the rest of the world? Post-paper-clip questions such as these have served me well. Perhaps they even made me a writer.

For wherever there is a secret, there is a story. . . .

Lisa Rowe Fraustino
October 11, 1997

BY BRUCE COVILLE

The Secret of Life, According to Aunt Gladys

"Your brother called this afternoon."

This seems like a fairly simple sentence. Yet when Dad uttered it at the dinner table last April, it caused my mother to turn pale and freeze, holding her broccoli-laden fork halfway to her mouth.

I felt as surprised as she looked. "I didn't know you had a brother," I said, watching her fork to see if the broccoli would fall off. "What's his name?"

"George," said Mom. She sounded as if she was having a hard time getting the word past her throat, and I don't think she was really answering my question. "George called?"

Dad nodded.

"What did he want?"

"He said he's coming for a visit."

The fork, broccoli still attached, hit the plate. "*What?*"

"He said he's coming for a visit."

"Who's George?" I asked.

"Your mother's brother," said my father.

"I know *that*," I replied. "At least, I know it now. How come I didn't know before?"

"We don't talk about George," said Dad. From the look in his eye, I got the feeling he was enjoying this.

"Why not?"

"Randy, if I wanted to tell you that, we would have talked about him before," said Mom sharply. Turning to my father she said, "Did you tell him not to come?"

"He's your brother," said Dad, which wasn't quite an answer but seemed to provide the necessary information, at least if the tightening in Mom's jaw was any indication.

"Did he leave a number?" she asked.

"Nope."

She narrowed her eyes. "Did you even ask?"

"Actually, I did," said Dad, obviously pleased that he was off the hook on this one. "But he said he was traveling and didn't have a number where he could be reached."

My mother picked up her plate and left the table.

"What's the matter with her?" I asked, once she was gone.

"She doesn't like George."

"Thanks for the news flash, oh fatherly fountain of wisdom. Care to tell me *why* she doesn't like George?"

"Actually, I don't have the slightest idea. All I know is that George has been the Great Unmentionable ever since I met your mother. I only found out about him myself because I saw a picture of him in an album at your grandmother's house."

Mom's mother, Gramma Verbeck, lives about three thousand miles from us, in a little town in Maine. I've only been to her place twice, so it was no surprise that I hadn't found out about George through her.

2

Then I realized this guy wasn't just George to me. From my point of view he was *Uncle* George. This was a very interesting thought. I have three aunts—one on Mom's side, and two on Dad's—but I never had an uncle before, at least not one that I knew about. I had always kind of wanted one, though. From what I had seen, they were pretty good things to have. For example, Spud Martin gets to live at his uncle's camp in the mountains every summer. Well, Spud's uncle is rich, so maybe that doesn't count. But Peter MacKenzie's uncle is always taking him to ball games, and Herb Lassiter's uncle hangs out and plays two-point in the driveway with us sometimes. So all in all, uncles seemed like a good idea.

Except, from the way my mother was acting about Uncle George, you'd think the guy was a baby-eater or something.

I was getting ready to ask Dad some more questions when the doorbell rang.

"See who that is, find out what they're selling, and then tell them we don't want any," said Dad. "I have to go talk to your mother."

I crammed another bite of casserole in my mouth and went to the front door. It was open, because it was a nice night and we had wanted to let the breeze in, so there was only a screen door between me and the tall, elegant-looking woman standing on the porch. A big sample case sat next to her.

"What are you selling?" I asked, eyeing the case and not even making a move to open the door.

"Etiquette lessons would seem appropriate," she replied in a husky voice. "You must be Randy."

"I narrowed my eyes. "How do you know that?"

Before she could answer, my mother shrieked, "George! Get off that porch before the neighbors see you!"

And that was how I met my uncle George.

———

3

The idea that this was my long-lost, or at least long-misplaced, uncle was a bigger lump than Mom's broccoli casserole. I was still trying to digest it—the idea, not the casserole—when George said, "I can't get off the porch until someone opens the door."

"Yes you can," said Mom. "Just turn around and walk away."

"Are you serious?" asked George. His lower lip trembled, and I thought for a minute he was going to cry. I backed away from the door, not particularly wanting to watch his mascara run.

"Of course I'm serious!" sputtered Mom. "If you think—"

She stopped as Dad put his hand on her elbow and began to whisper in her ear.

She closed her eyes and sighed; her spine, which had been as rigid as a telephone pole, seemed to collapse. "All right, George," she said softly. "You can come in."

"Randy," said Dad, "go unlock the door for your uncle."

I did, then stepped back, not wanting George to touch me. I felt like I did back in third grade, when I still thought cooties were real. At the same time, I was wondering if maybe this would be enough to get me on one of those daytime talk shows.

When George came through the door, I realized that what I had thought was a salesperson's sample case was actually his suitcase.

The realization hit Mom at the same time. "Now look," she said, "If you think for one minute—"

Before she could finish, George drew himself up to his full height, which was considerable. Looking her right in the eye, he said in a low voice, "When I was naked you clothed me, when I was hungry you fed me."

I recognized the words. They're from a speech Jesus makes somewhere in the New Testament. George was either very smart, or very devious—or very religious, which didn't seem likely under the circumstances. (Actually, it turned out that he is religious, which still sort of surprises me.) Anyway, he sure knew the way to get to Mom. She is a Very Serious Church Person, serious enough not to be a hypocrite, once she thinks about things. For the second time in as many minutes I could see the wind go out of her sails.

She closed her eyes, then said softly, "What do you need, George?"

"Gladys," said George.

"You need Gladys?" I asked, surprised at the thought.

"Gladys is my new name," replied George, with a surprising amount of dignity. "And what I need is a place to stay while I finish having my surgery."

Without intending to, I crossed my legs.

Mom staggered a little, and Dad helped her to the couch.

"We're going to be sisters!" said George, and though his voice was cheerful, I caught a kind of desperate eagerness in his eyes.

I was starting to get desperate, too. Though I had been amused at my mother's reaction, I was beginning to wonder what the guys were going to say about this. I was also wondering how much Spud Martin would charge to swap uncles.

"Well, isn't anyone going to ask me to sit down?" asked my would-be aunt.

"Sit down . . . Gladys," said my father.

"Why thank you," said George/Gladys. Settling to the couch, s/he crossed his/her clean-shaven legs at the knees. S/he carefully straightened a panty-hose wrinkle, then looked around and said, "Well, isn't this *nice?* A genuine family gathering!"

My mother made a small, strangled sound. George/Gladys was definitely not her idea of family. Actually, Mom's idea of a family is very simple: one man and one woman get married, and they have kids. That's it. End of choices. In the world according to Mom, no one gets divorced, no one has affairs, and for God's sake no one even *imagines* being any sex other than the one they started out as!

5

Mom brought up that exact point a little later in the conversation. "Listen, George," she said severely, "God made you the way you are for a reason."

"If She made me this way for a reason, perhaps the reason was to test your love and tolerance," replied George/Gladys primly.

"Don't be ridiculous! I mean God made you a man for a reason. And don't call God a her!"

"Do you really believe God purposely put me into a body where *He* knew I would be permanently miserable just to test me? Is that any more ridiculous than thinking the test was to see if I would have the courage to do something about it? You don't know God's will, Ginny. None of us do. So you might as well stop fussing about trying to tell me what it is, and just decide if you're going to keep on being my sister or not. After all, that was God's will, too."

Mom stood up. "You can stay here until this is over, George, if you absolutely have to. But we are not going to talk about it, not now, not ever. And no one else is going to know about it! I don't want the neighbors gossiping about this. It's a secret." Turning to me, she added, "Is that clear, Randy?"

"Hey, you think I want this to get around?" I asked, putting my hands up. "My life in school is hard enough as it is. No offense, George. Er, Gladys."

"It's *George*," said my mother sharply, "And will be as long as *he's* in the house. Is that clear, George?"

"Clear, but highly offensive," replied George softly.

"Those are the terms."

He bent his head. "Terms accepted, Sis. May I be excused? From the room, I mean."

They put him in the spare bedroom at the end of the hall.

"Now you stay away from him, Randy," said Mom in a fierce whisper, once George's door was safely closed. "And for heaven's sake, don't let him try anything with you."

"Mom!" I said, totally disgusted.

"Well, you can't be too careful."

I suspect that's not actually true. I think you can be way too careful. You can be so careful that you go your whole life without ever seeing a rainbow because you're so busy trying not to step in any puddles.

The next couple of days were not easy. To begin with, the emotional temperature in our house dropped by about fifty degrees. And I was a nervous wreck at school, torn between a desperate need to talk to someone, *anyone*, about what was going on in my house, and a desperate fear that someone would actually find out. I could think of several guys, including Spud Martin, who would cheerfully use that information to make my life a living hell.

I almost told Moonglow, who is sort of my girlfriend, one afternoon when we were walking home after school. (Moonglow's real name is Heather, but she changed it because she said it wasn't really her. So I thought maybe she would understand.)

We were walking along, holding hands, and I said, "Was it hard when you decided to change your name?"

I thought this might give me a good opening. But after she thought about it for a minute, she said, "Nah. It's not like I was changing my sex, or something."

Which pretty much made me decide this wasn't the time to talk about Uncle George. What if she thought it was something that runs in the family?

Besides, comparing what George was doing to changing your name was like comparing an alligator to a salamander.

The only thing that improved around the house after that first night was our meals. This was because Uncle George started doing the cooking, and he was a lot better at it than Mom. But even that had its downside, since I don't think it did anything to make her any happier about the situation.

The third night after George's arrival I was sitting at the dining room table doing my homework when he came in, sat down opposite me, and started to file his nails. He was wearing a dark-blue blouse, jeans, and full makeup. Actually, I never saw him without his makeup.

Neither one of us said anything for a while. Finally he brushed back his hair—revealing a dangling earring—and asked, "What are you working on, Randy?"

"Biology," I replied. Immediately I wished that it had been any other subject.

George smiled. "Me, too."

My discomfort must have shown on my face, because George laughed—such an easy, open laugh that I couldn't help but smile myself. I closed the book and looked at him. "I can't believe I had an uncle all this time and never knew it."

"I suppose I would come as sort of a shock," said George, shrugging his shoulders, which were a little too wide for his blouse. "Especially now."

"You're not kidding. Just finding out you existed would have been surprise enough for one week. Much less all the—all the rest of it."

George made a face. "I don't make things easy, do I?"

"So, how long have you . . . ?" I trailed off, uncomfortable with the question.

"How long have I been a family secret?" filled in George.

Actually, I had been going to ask how long he had been working on turning into a woman, but this question was almost as interesting. So I nodded. "Yeah, how long?"

He pursed his lips. "Hard to say. I can't remember a time when the rest of the family didn't disapprove of me. Oh, I guess they loved me when I was a babe in arms. But from the time I was old enough to start being interested in things, and it turned out that all the things I was interested in were for girls, not boys, they tried to keep a lid on me. Not that it worked that well. I mean, you are what you are, you know? But I got pretty well smacked around for it. Not by Dad," he added quickly. "By my fellow classmates. A charming bunch of thugs, much approved of by most of the town."

His voice was very calm, but I noticed that his hand was trembling.

"It would have been one thing if Dad helped me out with the beatings—given me sympathy or advice, or talked to the parents of the kids who were doing it. But he never did. I think he figured if I got beat up enough I would straighten out." He spread his hands in helpless disbelief. "Good grief, if it was that easy I would have turned butch the first time I got the crap kicked out of me for being a 'sissy.' How Dad could think I would insist on acting in a way that made my life so difficult if I had a choice . . ."

Suddenly he turned away. When he turned back I could see tears trembling in the corners of his eyes.

"Sorry, Randy. I get a little emotional sometimes." He chuckled. "I'd claim it's because the doctors are having trouble balancing my hormones, but the truth is I've always been like this." He took a deep breath. "Anyway, as I got older the teasing and whispering and jokes and fights just kept getting worse. When it all got to be too much, I ran away from home."

"How long did you stay gone?" I asked, remembering the times I had run away myself. I think four hours was my personal best.

"I never went back."

9

"Never?"

He shook his head firmly.

"How old were you?"

"Fourteen."

"How did you live?"

He looked away. "You do what you have to do. I did get a little help from your mother. She was the only one in the family I stayed in contact with."

"You're talking about my own personal mother?" I asked. "The one sitting in the next room?"

"Her heart is a lot kinder than her mouth," said George.

I thought about that for a minute. "Yeah, I guess maybe you're right," I said at last.

After that neither of us said anything for a while. When the silence started to feel uncomfortable, I said, "Want to give me a hand with this homework?"

He smiled as if he'd just won the lottery. "What do you want me to do?"

"Ask me these chapter questions," I said, passing him the book.

I got an A on the chapter test the next day, the first I'd managed in biology all year long.

"Hey, Randy!" said Spud Martin, as we were leaving class. "What happened, you get a brain transplant or something?"

"I just studied more than usual," I mumbled, ashamed to mention George, afraid what the conversation would lead to.

I was also ashamed of being ashamed. I remembered something Jesus said to Peter, the night before he was crucified. "You will betray me three times before the cock crows."

And sure enough, Peter did.

When I used to hear that story in Sunday School, I always thought

Peter was a real creep for not speaking up when people asked if he knew Jesus.

I always told myself that I wouldn't have been such a coward.

But this was different.

At least, that's what I told myself now.

I wasn't the only one having a hard time admitting that George existed. While Mom's heart may have been kinder than her mouth, she did a good job of not letting that kindness show over the next few days.

"George," she would say, out of the blue, "have you thought about the fact that this is going to kill Mother if she finds out?" Or, "Can't you have a little consideration for anyone else, George? Why is it only what *you* want?"

That was when she talked to him at all.

Maybe it was because she was being so mean to him that I started talking to him more myself. He never "tried anything" with me, as Mom so delicately put it. But he did tell me things I doubt she really wanted me to know. Not about his upcoming operation—that was something I was trying hard to *not* think about. (I mean, really . . .) Mostly it was stuff about our family history.

He even had a photo album, which he brought so he could show me some of the people he was talking about. When I asked him how come he was dragging around an album filled with pictures of people who hadn't treated him all that well, he replied, "There's a difference between leaving and forgetting, Randy. Leaving is the easy part."

Things in our immediate family reached the boiling point the night before George was to go in for his surgery. Dad had an important meeting of some sort, so it was just Mom, George, and me at dinner, which wasn't all that comfortable, especially since Mom was acting kind of funny. I figured out why after dessert, when she said, "Mrs. Patchett from next door is coming over in a little while to talk about the church supper we're organizing for next week."

"That will be nice," said George, who was clearing the table. "Would you like me to make a fresh pot of coffee?"

"What I want you to do," said Mom in a steely voice, "is stay in your room. I do *not* want Margaret to see you."

George's cheeks flamed red. He didn't say a thing, though; just set the plates he was holding in the sink and left the room.

"Nice work, Mom," I muttered.

"Don't you start, Randy!" she snapped.

"I've got homework to do," I said, shoving myself away from the table.

It was true. I did have homework to do. But I couldn't concentrate on it, especially when I heard Mom and Mrs. Patchett nattering away down in the living room. Finally I went up to George's room. When I knocked on the door, he pulled it open so quickly it startled me. He had on the same outfit he had been wearing the day he arrived, and he was holding his suitcase.

"What are you doing?" I asked.

"Leaving."

"Don't!" I said, astonishing myself.

"Why not?"

"Because you still need someplace to go while you're recovering," I said, surprised at how important it was to me that he not go.

"I can't stay here, Randy. Not if I have to be some sort of horrible secret. I know that was the agreement. But I just can't do it."

He started past me. I grabbed the suitcase from his hand and walked back into his room with it. I plunked it onto the bed and opened it. Trying not to look at the lacy underwear, I pulled out the photo album he had showed me.

12

"Take this downstairs," I said, thrusting it into his hands. "Tell her what you told me."

"Why?"

"Because if you go now, she's not going to change. And you need her to change, George. *I* need her to change. It might not work. But it's the only chance either of us has. I don't think she knows the stuff you told me. If she knows it, she doesn't think about it."

He glanced at the door.

"Leaving is the easy part," I said.

George sighed. He stared at me for a long moment, then nodded and took the album from my hands.

I followed him down the stairs, and into the living room.

Mom gasped when we walked in. Mrs. Patchett put down her coffee cup and smiled, clearly waiting for an introduction.

"What is it, Geo . . . *Gladys?*" asked Mom.

"We have to talk," said George in a surprisingly deep voice. (I could tell he had to work to keep it down there.)

Mrs. Patchett's eyes widened.

"Not now!" said Mom desperately.

"Yes, now," said George. "We need to talk about us, Ginny. About our family. About secrets."

Mom stood up. "I don't think—"

"That's the problem, at least part of the time," snapped George. "You *don't* think. You just go by the stuff our dear mother drummed into your head. Or you do think, but what you think doesn't have anything to do with what's real. Now sit!"

She didn't move.

"Sit!" he barked, sounding like a drill sergeant.

Mom sat. She turned to Mrs. Patchett with a desperate look on her face.

"Oh, don't mind me, dear," said Mrs. Patchett, looking as happy as I had ever seen her. She picked up her coffee cup. "I'll just wait while you two have your little chat."

George plunked the album down on the coffee table. Facing Mom, with the table between them, he knelt. Then he opened the album to the first page. "Our father," he said, pointing to a photo I had seen a hundred times. I had never actually met Grampa Verbeck; he died before I was born. But I almost felt like I knew him from that picture. He was wearing an army uniform, standing with his arms crossed, his head thrown back, an open smile on his face. Sometimes I check the mirror, hoping I will turn out to look like him.

"What about him?" asked Mom.

"How did he die?"

"You know very well how he died. He was killed in a terrible car accident. A truck ran a stop sign and—"

"Stop right there. The truck didn't run the stop sign, Dad did. He was dead drunk. And so was the teenage girl he had in the car with him."

"That's not true!"

"It most certainly is. I looked up the court records. I've got a copy, if you want to see them. The only place it isn't true is in our family, where we tried to keep it a secret."

Mom turned to me. "Randy, leave the room," she ordered.

"Stay right where you are!" snapped George.

"Tell her about Uncle Louie," I said eagerly.

George nodded and flipped forward a few pages. "Uncle Louie," he said, when he came to the right picture. "Know how many times he was married?"

"Once," said Mom firmly.

"Twice. He has two kids by his first marriage, but he pretends they don't exist. A pair of cousins that you never got to meet, Ginny."

"Stop, George. Please?"

"Not now," he said, his voice relentless. "It took me too long to get started." He turned the page. "Aunt Pam. Terrific lady. I like her a lot. Good marriage. Three great kids, one of them actually from her husband. She just got back from her third trip to detox."

He turned the page. "Ah. Mom."

"What about her?" asked my mother, her voice suddenly protective.

"She ever tell you about—"

"Stop it!" screamed Mom. "Stop it right now!"

"No, you stop, Ginny," he said fiercely. "Stop pretending. You want to keep me a secret because you think I'm the great disgrace of the family. But I'm not. I can take you back through a chain of horse thieves and hookers that would make your head spin. Generations of disgraceful behavior."

"My great-grandfather killed a man once," put in Mrs. Patchett hopefully. "Up in Alaska."

George rolled on as if he hadn't heard her. "But we kept all those things hidden. Then I came along, and somehow I couldn't master the trick of hiding. My little 'problem' ruined the illusion that we're normal."

He was starting to cry now, just a few tears leaking out of the corner of his eyes. He leaned across the coffee table and took my mother's hands. His voice low and urgent he said, "Listen, Ginny: *no one's family is normal,* at least, not normal like you use the word. All the 'good' people, the 'nice' people, they try to hide the messy parts of their lives and pretend that everything is just fine. And sometimes it even looks good on the surface. But all that hiding, it kills something in your heart.

"Yeah, I was a weird kid. So what? I didn't hurt anyone. Not like

Buzz Walker, most beloved person in the school. I kept track of them all after I left, you know. Even stayed in touch with a few people, including Margie Simmons, the girl Buzz raped."

Mrs. Patchett gasped and spilled her coffee.

"But Buzz was a hero," continued George. "So it got hushed up. Me, I was just the boy who liked to dress funny, so I didn't get hushed up, I got beat up. Sorry, just a trifle bitter there. But don't you see, Ginny? These secrets are like a slow poison, eating their way through our family, through our lives. And what do you get by hiding them—by hiding me? The respect of your neighbors?"

He glanced at Mrs. Patchett, who shook her head, wide-eyed, as if to say she would never respect someone who hid a secret.

"I guarantee you, Scout's honor, heart of gold, swear on a Bible, the neighbors are keeping secrets, too. The sad thing about it is, they're so busy trying to hide things that they're missing the real secret of life. But it's right out in the open. They'd see it if they'd just open their eyes. Do you know what it is, Ginny? Do you know the real secret of life?"

She shook her head.

"Then I'll tell you. Here it is: Normal is bigger than most of us think. Someone out there, I don't know who, is trying to shove us all into little boxes. 'This is all you can be,' they say. 'This is all you're allowed.' But it's a lie. People, real people, are bigger than that, stranger than that. You, me, Mom, Dad—our whole family—if you compare us to the tight little lie of what we're supposed to be, we're all whacked. But if you could see the truth, see everyone's truth, you'd know we're no weirder than anyone else. Even me. Even me, Ginny." He clutched her hands more tightly. "Don't turn away from me now, sister. Don't pretend I'm something you have to hide. I'm not evil. I'm *not!* I just want to be what I am!"

With that he fell forward, sobbing like a baby. Mom stared down at him for a moment, then lifted her hand to stroke his hair. "Poor Georgie," she whispered, tears running down her cheeks. "Poor baby brother."

Mrs. Patchett put down her coffee cup. "I think I'd better go," she said softly.

After she tiptoed out of the room I took her place on the couch.

I sat there until Dad came back, patting my mother on the shoulder with one hand, patting George with the other, trying to make sense of it all.

Aunt Gladys is coming home today.

I, for one, will be glad to see her, since it's been kind of dull around here without her.

Next week, when she's feeling better, I'm planning to introduce her to Moonglow.

And after that . . . well, after that I might tell my parents about what Coach Lewis did to me back in seventh grade.

I'm tired of keeping it a secret.

Besides . . . what's the point?

BY SUSAN CAMPBELL BARTOLETTI

Rice Pudding Days

Rice Pudding

½ cup butter   3 eggs

6 cups whole milk   ¼ to ½ cup sugar, depending upon taste

¾ cup rice   1 teaspoon vanilla

Melt butter in deep sauce pan. Add milk. When milk starts to boil, add rice and stir. Let milk simmer for about 20 minutes or until the rice has absorbed most of the milk. Beat eggs until thick. Add sugar to eggs and continue beating. To prevent the egg mixture from coagulating, add a little of the hot milk mixture to the eggs and stir. Then whisk all of the egg mixture into the milk and rice. Stirring constantly, return the pudding to full boil. Boil for one minute. Remove from heat and add vanilla. Let cool, then refrigerate.

Some mothers drink or smoke or shop when they're depressed, but not my mom. She makes rice pudding. I asked her about it once, but she just smiled and said it made her feel better, because it made her think of her mother, my grandmother, who died when I was a baby.

So when I got home from school and the first thing I saw was the yellow rice box sitting on the counter and Mom standing at the stove, absently stirring a pot, it didn't take a genius to figure out something was wrong. Which was good, because I'm no genius. My older brother Nick might be, but my sister Lizzie and I swim at the shallow end of the gene pool.

On tiptoe, I peered over Mom's shoulder. "Rice pudding?"

She sniffed and nodded, still stirring. I was in a rice pudding mood myself, thanks to the 62 percent I had gotten on my biology test, a test I had studied hard for.

"What's wrong?" I asked.

She didn't say. Instead she tapped the spoon against the side of the pan and set it on the spoon rest. She went over to the kitchen table and picked up an official-looking letter, and held it out to me. I recognized the gold seal at the top. It was a college acceptance letter. For her. From Keystone University.

"Wow," I said, hugging her. "That's great. Congratulations. You should be happy."

"Anna," said Mom, biting her lip, "your father doesn't know I applied."

"Oh." So that was it. I loved my father, but he could be a real Grinch at times. "Then it'll be a nice surprise," I told her, hoping I sounded cheerful enough.

She shrugged, not saying a word, and returned to the bubbling pot of pudding.

———

Ordinarily, dinner was the best part of the day for us Vankos, especially when Nick was home from college and we were all together.

But not tonight. More than anything, I wished Nick were home, telling one of his funny stories, making everyone laugh. It was as though a dark cloud had passed over everyone. I was sulking over my biology grade, Mom was edgy, and Lizzie was gloomy, too.

Lizzie's mood swings were nothing new since she had started going out with Michael. Why couldn't she see what everyone else saw: that the one great love of Michael's life was himself? Usually, Lizzie used her super powers to rub out guys like cigarette butts. What made Michael so different, I supposed, was his age. He was not your ordinary high school guy. He was a sophomore at the university.

We passed around the meat loaf, mashed potatoes, green beans, and applesauce, as Lizzie squeezed ketchup onto a scoop of cottage cheese.

Dad stared. "You're eating that?"

Lizzie gave him a sour look. "My jeans are tight."

"Those old things?" said Mom. "It's about time you outgrew them."

"They're my favorites," she said with a sniff. "All broken in the way I like them."

Dad scowled and changed the subject. "I've seen a couple of stray cats living in the field across the road. They've been getting into our garbage, scrounging for food. Something's got to be done."

"Cats?" I said excitedly.

Dad knew what I was thinking. "These aren't pets," he said. "They're wild."

"What do you plan to do?" asked Mom.

"I'm borrowing a couple of traps from somebody at work."

"Traps!" The thought horrified me. I had seen pictures of trapped animals, their paws caught in steel teeth. Some, I knew, even gnawed their own feet off, just to get free.

20

"Not that kind," said Dad. "Live traps. I'll catch the cats and take them to the animal shelter."

"Nobody's going to adopt grown cats," I protested. "They only want kittens. A shelter will put them to sleep."

"Anna, I can't help that. Something's got to be done. Most likely those cats don't have their shots. They can't be running around wild, breeding and causing trouble."

I looked to Mom for help, but to my dismay, she agreed with Dad. "Your father's right," she said, but her face told me how sorry she felt for the cats.

After dinner, Dad turned on the kitchen TV and flipped through the channels to find the news. Lizzie and I cleared the table. Mom set out dessert dishes and the bowl of rice pudding. Dad raised an eyebrow at the sight of the bowl and looked at me. I shrugged and reached for the pudding. Into my dish, I plopped one spoonful in honor of the biology test and added two more scoops in honor of the cats.

"The mail was interesting today," said Mom casually, her eyes meeting mine. "For starters, I got a birthday card and letter from Nick."

She went into the living room and returned with two envelopes, one with Nick's handwriting and one with raised gold lettering. I grabbed Nick's. I hadn't seen my brother since he returned to school after spring break in March, over a month ago. I devoured his news about his classes and friends, then handed the letter to Dad.

Mom stacked the dirty plates in front of Lizzie. "Your turn."

Lizzie's face scrunched in pain. "Can't Annie? I have a headache."

"No way, you hypochondriac," I said. "I did them last time, when you had shooting pains in your stomach." I knew all she wanted was to sneak upstairs to call Michael.

Mom handled our disagreement in her usual fashion: she ignored us. She scootched her chair closer to Dad's and pulled out the second letter. "Look what else came in the mail today. I've been accepted to Keystone."

"The university? You didn't tell me—" said Dad.

I cut him off. "A nice surprise, huh, Dad?"

Even Lizzie was impressed. "That's great, Mom."

Dad took the letter from Mom. Although I could tell he tried hard not to, he grimaced anyway as he looked it over. "Catherine, you know I wish you could do this," he said. "I really do. But we're so strapped with Nick's tuition bills. And then there's Lizzie the year after next." He folded the letter and looked earnestly at Mom. "Besides, you're going to be thirty-nine years old. By the time you finish a degree—"

"Oh, you!" Mom sputtered, fighting back tears. "I'll be thirty-nine tomorrow whether I go back to school or not. I'm not asking your permission. All I want is your support." She got up from the table, knocking her chair against the wall, and stormed from the kitchen.

Dad seemed genuinely shocked. His shoulders slumped, he looked helplessly from Lizzie to me. "What'd I say? All I did was point out the facts."

"You hurt her feelings," said my ever-perceptive sister. "At her age, a woman doesn't want to be reminded how old she is."

Dad's chair scraped against the floor as he stood. He left the table and the screen door banged behind him as he went outside. It was followed by another loud bang from his workshop door in the garage.

"Men," said Lizzie, scraping the pudding bowl. She licked the spoon.

"I thought you were on a diet," I reminded her.

"I am. Look how fat I am." She lifted her shirt and pinched the skin on her stomach. A whole micro-fraction of an inch worth.

"Wow. You're really fat."

"Even Michael has noticed." She picked up the stack of dinner plates and carried them over to the sink. She began to rinse each plate and put it in the dishwasher.

"Your eating habits are none of his business."

"He cares about me." She sighed. "Maybe something else is wrong," she said, thinking out loud. "I missed a period last month. That could be a sign of cancer, you know."

My sister *was* a hypochondriac. "Big deal," I said, rolling my eyes. "I missed mine for fourteen years."

"Oo," huffed Lizzie. She slammed the dishwasher shut, causing all the glasses and plates to clink inside. "You're impossible to talk to. You're so immature."

"Maybe you're pregnant," I joked. Even Lizzie couldn't be that stupid.

"Shut up," she said sharply—a little too sharply if you ask me—and I could tell she was sorry she'd even brought the subject up.

I felt a twinge of remorse. Maybe Lizzie did need someone to talk to. "I'm sorry. But maybe your cottage-cheese-and-ketchup diets are screwing up your system. That happens, you know. Why don't you tell Mom or go see a doctor?"

Lizzie shook her head sadly and pressed a dish towel into my hand. Call me a sucker, but I helped her with the dishes, pretending all the while to be interested in her chatter about Michael and some up-coming concert he had promised to take her to. Michael, in my opinion, was her only disease.

After the last pot was dried, I found Dad at his workbench, sorting through a can of nails. In the garage, Dad had a place for everything and everything in its place. All his tools were lined up according to size and function, sandpaper according to grade, and paint according to color and hue. Mom says Dad's so neat that when he gets up in the

23

middle of the night to go to the bathroom, he makes the bed. The only problem is, she's still in it.

"Aw, Annie," said Dad, when he saw me in the doorway. "I didn't mean to hurt your mother's feelings."

I knew he didn't. He'd never hurt her feelings on purpose; he was just being practical, as always. Talk about opposites: Dad was the sort to count change and keep a penny-perfect checkbook; Mom was the sort to overtip waitresses and round off the checkbook balance.

"Going back to school's important to Mom," I told him gently. "It's all she ever talks about when she's with Nick. She's always asking him about his classes and what he's learning. She even reads the books he buys for his courses."

I wasn't telling Dad anything that he didn't already know. A sad look crossed his face. "Your mother thrives on change. She can't even leave the furniture alone."

I grinned. "Did you see the living room? She did it again." Mom's habit of rearranging furniture was a common joke in our house.

He chuckled and nodded, then grew quiet. He dropped several nails into a can and wrote "2-penny" on the side. "What's wrong with things staying the way they are?" he said, and I knew he wasn't talking about living-room furniture. He wasn't even talking to me; he was talking to himself. "I don't understand why she feels she needs college." There was another pause. "I suppose it's my fault. We got married so young."

I knew all about that: Mom was nineteen and Dad was twenty-one. She had dropped out of college to marry him her sophomore year. Dad never went to college, because he had a good job with the county. He was in charge of checking the weights and measures in the various grocery stores and gas stations and other places where scales and pumps were used. Mom worked at a small weekly newspaper, where she took care of the advertising bills.

"She always talked about finishing college," Dad continued, "but then Nick came along."

I looked at my feet, so Dad wouldn't see me smile. Even though no one ever admitted it, I knew Mom and Dad got married when they did because she was pregnant with Nick. It didn't take nine fingers to figure that out.

Something outside caught Dad's eye. He leaned across his workbench to look out the window. "There's one of those cats again," he said, pointing off to the edge of the field across the road from our house.

I looked out the door in time to see a half-grown marmalade cat before it disappeared into the tall grass.

Dad set the can of nails on the shelf. "Tomorrow I'm setting the traps. But right now, I think I'll go talk to your mother."

"Good idea."

Dad turned off the light, and I pulled the door shut behind us. In the house, Mom was sitting alone in the dark in the living room. Dad sat beside her on the couch and whispered something. She leaned her head against his shoulder, and he stroked her hair.

Quietly, I opened the refrigerator, sneaked some leftover meat loaf, took it outside, and set it by the field where I had last seen the cat.

Lizzie and I shared a bedroom. When Nick first left for college, Lizzie had begged to have his room, but Mom refused, saying he would still need it when he came home on break, so we were stuck with each other.

I sat at my desk, flicked on the lamp, and took out the purple beaded earrings I had made for Mom's birthday. Gently, I picked one up, admiring the way the light glinted off the purple glass beads. It was an intricate design, one that took me days to get just right, but I knew

Mom would love them. I inspected the beads and wire, then put the earrings back in the box and tucked it away.

That's when I heard the soft sound of Lizzie's voice. I got up and opened the closet. She was sitting on the floor, surrounded by shoes, talking on the phone. From the way she was cooing, I knew she was talking to Michael.

"It's after nine o'clock," I reminded her. Dad was strict about school-night phone calls.

Lizzie shot me a dirty look and yanked the closet door shut. I picked up my biology notebook and flopped across my bed to study the anatomy of mammals. Mammals, I thought, should be admired from the outside, not inside out.

Suddenly, Mom's voice bounced up the stairs. "Just forget it," she said sharply, coming down the hall, past my room.

Dad followed her. Their bedroom door slammed shut after them. "What's the matter with you?" His voice boomed from behind the walls.

My stomach twisted the way it always did when they argued. Poor Dad. I wondered what dumb thing he had said now. I didn't want to listen, but I couldn't help it. Biology notes couldn't drown out their argument.

"There's nothing the matter with me," I heard Mom say, her voice shrill. "Just leave me alone. I just want to be left alone."

Their voices fell, but the hushed tones still had sharp edges. After a while, Dad trooped past my room, a pillow tucked beneath his arm. He plodded down the stairs. There was a dull thud, and I knew he had walked into something. "Damn furniture," he shouted, and I could hear him jumping around. "Can't anything be left in one place?"

I switched off the light, crawled between the sheets, and pressed my face against the pillow. I could still hear the murmur of Lizzie's voice. I rolled over and thought about Mom's birthday. I hoped she

26

and Dad would make up so her day wouldn't be spoiled. Then I thought about the earrings again and hoped she'd like them. If she does, I thought with a yawn, I'll make her a matching necklace for Mother's Day.

The next thing I knew, Lizzie was pushing up the bedroom window. I sat up. "Lizzie!"

"Shut up," she said. "You'll wake everybody up."

"Where are you going?"

She didn't say. "Just leave the window open so I can get back in." She stuck one leg and her head out the window.

"Wouldn't the front door be easier?"

She folded the other leg through then stuck her head back in. "Can't. Dad's on the couch."

Her feet scraped along the porch shingles. The trestle rattled, then her feet hit with a light plop as she jumped to the ground. Straining my ears, I heard a distant car door slam and music play, then the sound of gravel being chewed up and spit out as the car pulled away.

I had no idea when Lizzie returned, but the next morning the shade was drawn, the window was closed, and she was curled in her bed, sound asleep. Her jeans lay bunched on the floor as if she had jumped out of them.

"Liz," I said. "Wake up. Time for school."

She mumbled.

I shook her shoulder, wishing I could somehow shake real sense into her. "Get up."

"Lemme alone. I don't feel good." She buried her head beneath the pillow.

Disgusted, I went downstairs. The couch was empty. At one end, a blanket was neatly folded beneath a pillow. In the kitchen, a birthday card sat propped in the center of the table. I smiled at Dad's signature and the XXs and OOs and all the words he had underlined for emphasis. No doubt about it: my parents had made up before work.

I ate breakfast, showered. Lizzie was still asleep, so I dug through her drawers for a shirt to wear. She didn't even stir. Usually her radar sounded whenever I borrowed her clothes without asking. Maybe she *was* sick, I decided.

I was nearly out the door when I remembered the cats. I back-tracked to the kitchen, rifled through the pantry cupboard, and found a can of tuna. I opened it, scraped it into a plastic container that Mom wouldn't miss, and carried it outside.

The marmalade cat and another gray tiger cat were playing, pouncing on each other and tumbling in the dirt. The orange cat spied me and broke away, hunkering low in the grass.

"Here, kitties," I called.

Slit-eyed and wary, the marmalade cat looked through me in that way that only cats can do. I held the tuna out. The two cats were so thin their bones showed. Slowly, I approached, coaxing them. "Here," I urged them. "It's for you."

The gray tiger scurried into a culvert near the edge of the field. I set the dish down, stooped, and looked inside. A black-and-white cat sprang to her feet, her back hunched and her eyes bright and round. She had puffed herself out to double her size. A low rumble came from her throat.

Startled, I backed off. Then I heard the tiniest mews. I looked again, as closely as I dared. Four tiny heads on four tiny bodies bobbed feebly.

"Kittens!" I exclaimed. The mother cat growled again. "Don't worry," I told her. "I won't hurt your babies," I pushed the tuna closer.

If she or the other cats were hungry, though, they didn't let on. I soon saw why as I looked back across the road to the other side of our garage, where Dad had set out the garbage earlier. The can was tipped. The garbage looked as though it had exploded.

Nearby, the orange cat was preening himself. He looked proud of his work.

"Gross," I muttered. "Is this the thanks I get?" Knowing Dad would have a fit if he got home from work later and saw the mess, I dropped my backpack and hurried to scoop up what garbage I could before the school bus arrived. I tossed a ketchup bottle, eggshells, and soup cans back into the garbage can. I picked up a cereal box then a smaller crushed blue-and-white box and started to throw both in, when my eyes caught the blue words on the white label. *Clear-n-Easy Home Pregnancy Test.*

Home pregnancy test. What was *that* doing in our garbage? I wondered, turning the box over. "Pink for positive," the label promised. Gingerly, I opened the box and took out the test stick.

It was definitively pink.

"Oh, Lizzie," I cried. "How could you be so stupid?"

The school bus rattled down the road, its yellow lights flashing. I pounded the lid securely onto the garbage can, grabbed my backpack, ran down the driveway, and climbed inside the bus. Feeling numb, I took the first empty seat and sat with my head against the window, a million questions jouncing inside my head.

Did Mom and Dad know about Lizzie?

Probably not. Our house still had a roof.

What would Lizzie do?

Would she marry Michael?

The thought of Michael as a brother-in-law made me shudder. There had to be something likeable about him, but I couldn't stand being around him long enough to find out.

29

Would she finish high school?

That didn't seem to be a problem. Every year our school had a few girls who looked as though they were stealing basketballs. There was even talk about offering day-care services for the babies so moms could attend classes. Some people railed against the idea, as if having day-care would encourage more girls to get pregnant.

My poor, stupid sister.

Stupid, stupid sister.

Just as tears began to spring to my eyes, we arrived at school. I didn't want my friends to see me crying, so I wiped my eyes on Lizzie's shirt, blew my nose, and forced myself to be cheerful.

It was the longest day of my life, thanks to biology class, where we discussed the gestation period of various mammals. I stared at the illustrations of human babies. Images of Lizzie and the home pregnancy test, pink for positive, turned in my head.

The reality hit hard: there was a baby no larger than my thumbnail growing inside my sister. I pored grimly over each picture, looking at how the baby would develop month by month, from something that looked like a tadpole to a baby complete with fingers and toes. I wished I could stop thinking about how the baby got there. The sex part, I mean.

Finally, it grew too much for me. I asked for permission to leave the room, ran down the hall to the lav, and cried myself out.

Later, I stepped off the school bus just as Dad was getting out of his car. He was whistling cheerily and holding a white bakery box. "Hey, Annie," he called to me. "Look at what I've got." He flipped open the lid to show off a pretty pink-and-white birthday cake inside.

"Mm," I said, hoping I sounded more cheerful than I felt. "Lots of junk icing."

"And extra roses," said Dad, winking at me. "You know how much your mom likes the roses."

Just like the roses on baby booties, I thought grimly, and I felt the tears starting all over again. To hide them I threw my arms around Dad and hugged him.

"Hey," he said. "What's that for?"

"No reason," I mumbled. I drew back and followed him across the patio and into the kitchen.

Mom was sitting at the kitchen table, sipping a cup of tea. When she heard us, she looked up. Dad and I both gasped and stopped short at the sight of her. Her hair was short—shockingly short—and pushed behind her ears.

Her hand flew to the back of her head, and her fingers pulled at the fringes, as if by pulling she could make them longer. "It's my birthday present to myself." She looked earnestly at Dad. "It's awful, isn't it?"

"Uh, no, it's, uh, different." Dad wriggled his eyebrows suggestively at her. "You're another woman."

Mom smiled shyly. "It's going to take some getting used to."

Dad circled his arms around her and pretended to bite her neck. "I'll say," he murmured. "I never realized what a pretty neck you have."

It was true. Mom's neck was like a swan's. But mostly I noticed her ears and how perfect they were for my earrings.

Looking embarrassed, Mom struggled to get out of Dad's hold. She pressed her hair into place.

Lizzie came downstairs and squealed—a little too cheerily for someone in her condition, if you ask me—when she saw Mom. "Your hair! I love it."

I couldn't help but stare at Lizzie's stomach in her too-tight jeans and short cropped T-shirt, as if I expected it to inflate any minute.

Mom forced a small smile.

After supper, we all sang "Happy Birthday," and Mom blew out the candles. Nick had sent Mom a new book from one of his classes, and Lizzie gave her a pretty scarf.

Mom oohed and aahed at each present, but I knew she was forcing herself to sound enthusiastic. Even though she was sitting there, with us, I could tell from the distant look in her eyes that her mind was a million miles away.

I handed Mom my present, wrapped in the comic section from the newspaper. She pulled off the paper and gasped at the earrings. "They're beautiful," she said softly. Right away, she put them on. As she turned her head from side to side, the earrings sparkled in the light, like a purple stained-glass window.

"How do they look?" she said.

"Great," said Lizzie. "Especially without all that hair in the way."

Mom squeezed the both of us.

Dad handed Mom a brightly wrapped box. She slid the ribbon off and peeled the paper back slowly. "Wonder what color blouse Dad got Mom this year," whispered Lizzie to me. I gave her a kick under the table.

Mom pried the lid off, then looked at Dad, a quizzical expression on her face, as if she didn't understand.

"What is it?" asked Lizzie eagerly, leaning in for a closer look.

Mom's hands trembled as she pulled out a Keystone University tote bag. It was stocked with Keystone pens, notebooks, folders, a sweatshirt, and a catalog.

"For school," said Dad. "I figured you'd need them."

Mom blinked and swallowed hard. "But the money—"

"Never mind that." Dad looked sheepish. "I've looked into cashing in part of a retirement policy."

"You what?"

He repeated what he'd said.

Mom bit her lower lip and her face scrunched, as if she were about to cry. She threw her arms around his neck. "Hold me," she said. "Hold me tight. And don't ever let go."

There was a time when Lizzie and I would have gagged and hollered "gross," but we were too old for that now. My sister and I grinned at each other.

After the party, Lizzie spent an extra long time getting ready to go out, then sat in the living room, twirling her hair around her finger, pretending to be interested in the news as she waited for Michael.

I had to admit it, Lizzie looked great. "Special date?" I asked, plopping down beside her on the couch.

She nodded happily. "Tonight's the concert at the university." Each time a car approached, she flew to the window. From the kitchen, Mom kept glancing in at us and whispering to Dad.

It wasn't the first time that Michael had failed to keep a promise, and I wished I knew what to say to her. But this was one of those no-win situations. If I cursed Michael, she'd defend him; if I made excuses for him, she'd tell me there weren't any.

I sat there, thinking of a million painful tortures for Michael. How could anyone be so cruel? Who did he think he was? Why did he break promises the way he did? Especially now, with Lizzie in this condition. Michael had the timing of a zit.

Unless—a horrible thought crept my head—maybe he knew about the baby. Maybe the baby was the reason he wasn't here.

Oh God, what kind of a father would he be?

Probably the kind of deadbeat dad you heard about on the news.

I guess I looked sorry-eyed at Lizzie once too often, because she snapped at me, "Don't look at me like that. I'm sure he has a good reason for being so late."

33

"Yeah," I said. "Maybe he's had an accident." I wondered if I sounded too hopeful.

Lizzie sat there, never saying a word, just wiping her eyes and swallowing hard. Finally, at nine o'clock, puffy-eyed, she went upstairs.

It was time for the moment of truth. I needed to know everything— about the baby, about Michael, about Lizzie's plans. I had a right to know. After all, we were family. Families are supposed to discuss things, make decisions together.

For some reason, I thought of the mother cat, how she had puffed herself up to twice her size to protect her babies. Well, I was Lizzie's sister, ready to puff myself up to protect her. I could help her talk to our parents. She was my sister, and I was the baby's aunt. Aunt Anna.

I went upstairs and found Lizzie sprawled across her bed, her face buried in tissues. From the looks of the soggy pile next to her, she had cried halfway through an entire box.

"You can tell me, Liz," I said, lowering myself next to her on the bed.

She blew her nose and fumbled for another tissue. "Tell you what?"

"About you and Michael."

Lizzie blotted her eyes, leaving dark smudges of mascara. "That jerk. Don't even mention his name. I hate him."

She honked again and discarded the tissue in the soggy pile.

"What are you going to do?"

She flopped back onto the bed and wailed into her pillow. "I don't know. He said he loved me."

I kneaded the back of her neck, the way Mom did when we were little. "Does he know about the baby?" I asked softly. I said it. It was out in the open.

There was silence. Dead silence.

"Baby? What baby?"

34

"I know, Liz," I said softly.

"You know what?" Then it dawned on her. She picked her head up and looked at me incredulously. Man, were her eyes bloodshot. "You think I'm pregnant?" Her mouth opened even further. "You think Michael and I—"

My heart was beating furiously. "Didn't you? I mean, aren't you?"

Lizzie stared at me. "Anna, I'm not pregnant. In order to get that way, you have to have sex. My God, give me a little credit, will you?" She sat up. "Sure, I like to sneak out and party and have a good time, but nothing else."

She snuffled some more. "That's why Michael and I have been fighting so much lately. He says our relationship is ready for the next step, and that means sex. All he cares about are his 'needs,' which means he doesn't care about mine at all." There was a pause. "Whatever gave you the idea I was pregnant?"

But I was only half listening. If Lizzie wasn't pregnant, then it must be—"Oh my God," I said.

"What?" said Lizzie. "What?"

I shook my head. "Nothing," I mumbled. "I'm . . . I'm sorry."

Lizzie looked at me as if I had two heads. Feeling dazed, I left the room and went into the bathroom, where I ran the tub water as hot as I could stand it. I undressed and climbed into the bath, sinking up to my chin. I stared at the tiled ceiling, letting the water swell around me, thinking about Mom. Part of me was excited at the thought of a baby, yet another part felt sorry. I thought about her birthday presents from Dad. I knew how badly she wanted to go back to school. What would she do now?

If only this tub was a bowl of rice pudding.

Usually weekends speed by, and before you know it, it's Monday, and you're back in school, wishing for Friday again. But not this weekend.

Lizzie spent most of the time in our bedroom, sulking, playing sad songs, and sniffling a lot. Mom was edgy and tense. Dad spent most of each day at his workbench. The traps lay in the field, carefully baited with cheese and lunch meat. I took extra good care of the cats, springing the traps, sneaking additional leftovers from the house, wishing the mother cat would trust me enough to let me hold one of her kittens.

On Monday, when I got home from school, Mom was on the phone. "Please check again," she said, a quaver in her voice. "Maybe there's something." She leaned her head against the wall and was twirling the cord in tiny jump-rope circles. Her eyes had purple crescents behind them. "Friday?" she said in a small voice. "Three o'clock. Yes. I'll take it."

She held onto the receiver until it beeped loudly as a reminder to hang up.

"You okay?" I asked.

Startled, Mom quickly washed her hands over her face. When she turned to me, her face looked pinched, ready to cry.

"I'm fine," she said, dumping a cup of rice into a pot.

I tipped my head toward the pot. "Then why the pudding? Did you and Dad have another fight?" Please, I thought, tell me about the baby.

"No," she said sharply. "Can't a person just be hungry?"

Her voice had an edge to it, but when she looked at me, her eyes melted a little. "I woke up with the strangest feeling today. I felt like calling my mother. I wish I could talk to her." Mom bit her lip.

I hugged her. "Talk to me." There. I was practically begging her.

But Mom didn't say a word. She kissed my forehead and squeezed me back. "I know. You're one great kid."

I threw myself into my schoolwork that week. I got an 86 percent on a biology quiz, which picked up my average a bit. My friends and I made sleepover plans for the weekend, and finally Friday rolled around again. When Lizzie and I got off the bus, I noticed the marmalade cat cleaning itself. It stopped and watched us intently. I'll get you some food, I promised him silently.

Lizzie and I went into the house. Mom and Dad weren't home, but a note was on the counter, telling us to fix macaroni and cheese for dinner. Lizzie immediately disappeared to our room. I turned the television on.

A news spot showed a group of protesters standing on a sidewalk, chanting and waving signs that read, "A baby has no choice" and "Abortion kills" and "Aren't you glad your mother didn't choose abortion?" One sign showed an unborn baby in a tear drop. It reminded me of the illustrations of the gestation periods in biology class.

A solemn-looking television reporter stood in the foreground. "Despite numerous requests by the police," she said, "the protestors have refused to leave the property, and several protestors who have blocked entry to the clinic have been arrested. Meanwhile, the clinic refuses to close its doors for today."

The reporter went on to give background information on abortion. Since it became legal, she said, over thirty million abortions had been performed.

Thirty million. It sounded like an enormous number, and I wondered who the thirty million women could have been. Were any of them people I knew—like friends or friends' sisters?

I reached to change the channel, but before I did, the camera shifted and focused on a woman who was being escorted by a police officer from the building. Hands shoved pamphlets at her. The woman, I figured, must have been a patient.

Her face was shielded, but the camera followed her, focusing on her departure through the crowd. The woman's hair was short, shaved in the back. Something caught in my throat then fell to my stomach as I recognized a neck as graceful as a swan's and one-of-a-kind purple beaded earrings.

The woman was my mother.

"No," I said. "Not my mother. My mother wouldn't do that. She couldn't do that."

The news spot was over now. I wished I could rewind it, to prove to myself there was some mistake.

But I knew there wasn't. No one else could have had those earrings.

My insides twisted. "So what if she was there? That doesn't mean—" I couldn't bring myself to say it.

"Oh, God." I wrapped my arms around myself, pressed myself against the kitchen wall, and slid to the floor.

All around me the kitchen, the television, the dishes, and the walls seemed to explode into bits of things, loud and soft, light and dark, bitter and sweet. I sat on the floor, hugging my knees.

Thirty million, the reporter had said.

I didn't know the thirty million, but I knew one.

My mother.

It seemed like hours before Mom's car pulled into the driveway. As she got out of the car, I thought how she didn't look like herself, with her hair cut so short and her neck so long and white. I couldn't stand to look at the earrings.

"Hi," she said when she walked through the door. "Sorry I'm late. Dinner ready?"

"No," I said. "Not yet." My mouth felt like straw.

"That's okay. I'm not very hungry."

Tell her, I said to myself. Tell her what you saw. Give her the chance to say it's not true, that it didn't happen, that somebody else's mother has purple beaded earrings.

But I didn't.

I looked at the tiny lines around Mom's eyes, and I wished I could read her mind. She poured herself a glass of orange juice, carefully, as though she was afraid to spill a drop.

She took one earring off and then the other and set them on the counter.

My eyes welled up. I couldn't stop myself. I went to her and hugged her tight.

"Bad day?" she asked softly. She stroked my hair without saying a word, the way she used to when I was little.

"The worst."

"I'm sorry."

I covered my mouth, afraid to look at her, because I knew she was crying. She didn't make any noise, but I knew she was, just the same. Her shoulders were hunched, and I could feel her shaking. I wanted to tell her that I loved her, but the words wouldn't come.

"My day wasn't so great either," Mom said. "I think I'll lie down a while." She scooped up her earrings from the counter and went upstairs.

Alone in the kitchen, I took out the yellow box of rice. Rice pudding. It was a recipe I had learned from my mother.

BY DIAN CURTIS REGAN

Words

Mellisa Meeker tapped on the door of her brother's bedroom. "Are you ready? Dad's bringing the car around."

No answer.

She peeked inside. Andy slumped on the edge of his bed, tie dangling from one hand, head resting in the other.

"Andy?"

He didn't move.

Puzzled, Mellisa stepped into the room. "Hey, big brother, what's wrong? Your fans await you. The whole town's coming to see its fave young writer receive the Tabor Medal."

She waited for Andy's typical smug smile, but he ignored her pep talk.

Whoa. This isn't the brother I know and envy.

She sat beside him. "Hey, Famous Senior." Flattery always worked.

Andy pulled his hand from his face. He looked awful—dark hair mussed, face red and splotchy.

Mellisa drew back. Had her self-assured brother been crying? "What? Are you nervous? The great orator of the Meeker family? Captain of the Whitman High Debate team? I could no more give an acceptance speech than—"

"Go."

His sharp response bit off the end of her sentence.

"Hey, it's me. I know your secrets and you know mine." She waited for him to acknowledge the reference to their late-night bonding sessions after Mom died. Dad had his own grief to deal with. All she and Andy had were each other—alone in the tiny apartment on the wrong side of town.

"*Leave,*" he insisted. "Tell Dad I'm riding to school with Jackson."

"Fine." Mellisa stepped to the door, hiding hurt feelings, waiting for him to grin at her and say, *Hey, I'm sorry. Case of nerves, that's all.*

But he didn't.

She strode down the dark-paneled corridor to the curved oak staircase, unable to descend this magnificent stairway without gliding down, pretending to be one of the many distinguished women who'd visited this mansion in years past. The mansion her family of the tiny apartment now called home.

At the bottom, she reverted back to Mellisa Meeker, daughter of Andrew Meeker III, granddaughter of Andrew Meeker II.

Andrew the second had built Meeker Mansion in the sixties. Oil money. That was the simple version of how her grandfather came into his fortune.

Mellisa pounded across the marble foyer and out the double front doors. Her father's rusty '89 Jeep idled in the curved drive. The Cadillac, inherited from his father, remained in the five-car garage.

Mellisa slid inside. "Andy's riding with Jackson," she explained.

Nodding, her father, the rebellious heir to the throne, released the emergency brake and took off.

Mellisa studied his profile as they rode along the quiet streets of Sinclair Hills. He acted annoyed at the posh neighborhood, insulted that his father had bequeathed him the mansion as well as a board position at Meeker Oil. Not what the anti-establishment, long-haired hippie, "I'm never going to be like you when I grow up" son had envisioned for a career. He'd done okay working for an environmental recycling firm until *downsizing* became a key word in the industry. How could a single dad—out of work with kids to support—remain a rebel?

"Look at all the cars," Dad exclaimed as they neared Whitman High. "This town sure comes out on award night to support its local sports heros."

Mellisa spotted the Channel 9 van. A satellite dish perched on top like a party hat. Even though most of the audience was here to cheer for Whitman's star athletes, she was proud of Andy for his literary win.

Shuddering at the sight of the news team and camera, Mellisa braced herself as Dad zigzagged into a parking spot. How could Andy address hundreds of people with a TV camera in his face? She would have melted into a puddle of self-consciousness.

Mellisa climbed from the Jeep. "I could *never* be the center of attention like Andy. I'm warning you, Dad, I won't amount to much."

She watched him lock the door, wondering how she felt about Andy being the perfect conformist son *his* father had wanted.

"Sure you will, Mell."

"Nope. Never going to win a Pulitzer or Nobel if it involves public speaking. Won't even try."

"Ha. I'm glad my daughter sets high goals for herself."

Mellisa looped an arm through his as they walked, marveling at the number of people streaming toward the auditorium.

Too bad Grandpa couldn't be here tonight. As a self-made man, he'd made up for his lack of education by filling Meeker Mansion with books—*three* libraries, plus a volume-filled garret above the east wing where he retreated whenever he wearied of being an oil baron.

How proud Grandpa would've been to know that Andrew Meeker IV had written a prize-winning collection of poems and prose in his beloved garret.

Mellisa often browsed the many bookshelves, but found no romances or science fiction adventures, just lots of biographies, history books, and classics—far too much *lit-tra-chure* for her taste.

Andy loved the libraries—probably because he'd wanted to be an author ever since fourth grade, when he wrote a goofy parody of "'Twas the Night Before Christmas" ("and all through the school, not a student was working or obeying a rule. . . .") The impressed teacher circulated copies—and Andy's reputation as a writer was launched.

Mellisa led her father into the auditorium. Mrs. Castano, the history teacher who'd taught at Whitman for at least a hundred years, was instantly beside them. "There you are," she exclaimed. "Seats for the award recipients and their families are down front."

Down front? Cool.

"Where is . . . ?" Mrs. Castano dipped her head to peer at the incoming crowd over her reading glasses.

"Andy's riding with a friend," Dad explained. "He'll be here in a minute."

Nodding, Mrs. Castano escorted them down the slanted aisle toward the stage. Part of Mellisa wished Andy was with them so everyone would recognize her as the Wonder Boy's sister. Another part was glad he wasn't. It let her be the anonymous sophomore that she was.

Front row left. Roped-off seats. Impressive.

Letter-jacketed jocks filled the rest of the front row. Already they were rowdy, ignoring Mrs. Castano's pleas to tone it down.

Mellisa studied the awards program: Welcome from Principal Osaka. Music by the Senior Chorale. Presentation of awards to the newspaper staff and outstanding members of various school clubs. *Then,* presentation of the Tabor Medal (to Andy!). Lastly, sports awards to the hotshots of Whitman High.

Ha, they saved the loudest awards for last.

On stage, Mr. Sampson, the English lit teacher, was testing the microphone and acting self-important. In the orchestra pit, Ms. Tooley, hustled band members to their places.

Where was Andy? Mellisa twisted in her seat to scan the aisles. It was almost time for the program to begin.

Feeling nervous for him made it hard to sit still. She tugged on Dad's sleeve to interrupt his chat with Andy's trig teacher. "I'm going to get a drink."

Out in the main hall, somebody thumped her on the head.

"Jackson, there you are." Mellisa gazed up at her brother's best friend. All six feet four inches of him. "Where's Andy?"

Jackson's dark eyes glinted. "He came with you."

Confused, she pictured Andy in his room, disheveled and depressed. Alarm made her clutch Jackson's sleeve. "No he didn't."

Jackson's amusement turned to concern. He jiggled his car keys. "Let's go get him."

Mellisa ran to keep up with Jackson's lanky strides. She *should* go back to tell Dad they were leaving, but the look on Andy's face when he'd ordered her from his room spurred her on.

Something must be terribly wrong.

The mansion was dark. Mellisa and Jackson raced through the foyer and up the stairs, clicking on lights as they ran.

Andy's room was empty. Mellisa's heart pounded as she snatched his crumpled tie from the floor.

"Meeker!" Jackson shouted down the hallway. "You here?"

Creaking from the thirty-year-old mansion was their only answer.

Jackson moved down the hall, opening doors to make sure every room was empty. "Why would he bolt, Mell? He craves the spotlight."

"I don't know." Fear made her voice tremble. She hated anything that upset her life. Mom. A new home. A new school. Too, too much.

Andy, what are you doing?

She followed Jackson down the hall, absently winding her brother's tie around her hand. "Did Andy say anything strange to you? Or act different?"

Jackson shrugged. "He gets moody sometimes. Who doesn't?"

The panicky feeling that consumed her after Mom died tightened Mellisa's chest. "We've got to find him," she said.

Jackson headed for the stairs. "You look up here. I'll search the main floor, and—"

"No."

"But you said—"

"There's only one place Andy could be."

Turning, Mellisa ran upstairs to the third-floor guest rooms. Jackson was on her heels. At the end of the hallway, she opened a narrow door, exposing a curved stairwell, paneled in dark mahogany.

She flipped on a light. The bulb blinked out with a foreboding *pop*.

"Where do these stairs go?" Jackson whispered.

"To my grandfather's garret."

Stumbling on the first step, Mellisa stopped. "Um, I need to go up alone."

"But why?"

"I—I just need to." Loyalty to her brother kicked in, making her

45

want to protect his ego. He never cried in front of anyone—not even at Mom's funeral. And only once in front of his little sister.

"Look," she began. "I know you guys are friends, but . . ." Hesitating, Mellisa tried to be tactful. "If Andy's up there, I think he'll be straight with me. If you're there, he may clam up. It's a guy thing, you know?"

Jackson looked wounded but stepped back as if he understood. Reaching into his pocket, he handed her a key chain. "Here's a flashlight in case you need it."

Mellisa crept up the dark stairway, aiming the mini-light at the steps. She'd been to the garret only once. At first she had thought she'd like the round room, because it reminded her of a high tower in a castle. But the floor to ceiling windows unnerved her. Beyond a narrow ledge was a sheer, four-story drop. Made her nervous. She'd never gone up there again.

Didn't bother Andy. He loved the garret enough to turn it into his writing room.

At the top of the circular stairs, a soft glow outlined the door. Clicking off the flashlight, Mellisa stepped inside, letting her eyes adjust to the dim lamplight. Her heart skittered when she realized the garret was empty.

A movement drew her attention to the far window.

Andy. Outside, sitting on the ledge.

Mellisa sucked in a breath. There was nothing between him and the concrete drive far below.

She moved slowly, not wanting to startle him.

"I knew you'd come back," he said dully, not bothering to turn around.

Mellisa's heart stalled. "Why are you out there?"

Twisting sideways, he scowled. "I think even a lowly sophomore can figure out why I'm out here."

"Touché," she muttered.

It was an old joke between them: lowly sophomores, conceited seniors. But this time, it wasn't funny.

She stopped three feet from the window. "Come inside," she demanded. Her fear of heights was new—sparked by images of her mother falling off a mountain to her death. The similarity of her brother's apparent intentions seemed beyond cruel.

"Why are you doing this to us?" To *me*, is what she really meant.

In the faint light, Andy's face scrunched in pain. "I'm not doing anything to *you*."

Anger heated her neck. Forget not showing up at school or not accepting his award. How *dare* he think of throwing himself off the mansion tower? How dare he think it would not affect her? Or Dad?

Her mind flashed back to the horrifying news from Alpine State Park where Mom had worked during tourist season. How her crampons had slipped on the sheer face of a cliff. How a rope had been tied improperly.

Falling.

Mellisa couldn't breathe. "Andy, why?"

"It's in the note," he blurted, motioning toward the desk.

Mellisa spotted the envelope on Grandpa's ink blotter. Dropping Andy's tie onto the desk, she opened the letter:

To the ones I leave behind,
The ones I hold most dear.
Remember me in softer times,
With friends and family near.

Before her mind could question if this mindless Hallmarky twaddle was the best he could do to say a permanent good-bye to his family, her gaze fell upon a line at the bottom of the page:

"Even these words are not my own, but Donovan Mueller's."

Mellisa glanced up at him, confused. "This doesn't tell me anything."

Exasperated, Andy swung around to sit sideways on the ledge.

Good, Mellisa told herself. *Talk him back inside.*

"Read between the lines!"

Mellisa flinched. Andy never yelled. She forced herself to stay calm. "Who is Donovan Mueller?"

"Look it up," he hissed.

With a sarcastic *tsk*ing, she motioned at the hundreds of volumes surrounding her. "So, where do I start?"

Cursing at her, Andy grasped the window frame and pulled himself inside.

Relief loosened the white-knuckled grip of her clasped hands.

Andy walked the stacks, trailing his fingers along book spines. Stopping, he yanked out the title he was searching for and flung it at her.

Mellisa dove to catch the heavy book, then flipped to the index. "Mueller, Donovan, page 1365." Finding the page, she scanned his bio. "He's an eighteenth-century writer. So what?"

"Look further."

She looked. "To the Ones I Leave Behind." Closing the book, Mellisa studied her brother's tense face. "You borrowed this guy's suicide note?"

"Think, Mell. I stole another writer's words."

"But you put his name on it."

Andy scoffed. "Yeah. *This* time I did."

The meaning of his words sank in. "You mean . . . the poems and stories you wrote for the Tabor competition? You borrowed words from other authors?"

Hanging his head, Andy turned away. "Borrowed. Stole. Same thing."

48

"How could you? You're a great writer. You don't have to—"

He waved a hand to silence her. Agitated, he paced across the garret, shirttail out. "I choked, Mell. Everybody expected me to win. Sampson was afraid some girl from Easton was going to take the medal. It's been six years since a Whitman student won. He was on some kind of mission. Kept hounding me. And . . . and I *tried*. But everything I wrote was drivel. I couldn't even show it to him."

While Andy talked, Mellisa casually circled the garret and lowered the window, careful not to look out. His words edged guilt into her mind. *How could I not have noticed that something was wrong?*

He's a good actor.

Andy straightened the reading lamp with a shaky hand. "Then there's Dad."

His voice quivered so much, Mellisa barely caught his words.

Andy glanced at her, as if hoping she wasn't listening. "Dad's already been humiliated by swallowing his pride and accepting Grandpa's inheritance. Plus losing Mom. How could I let him down by not winning?"

"*Forget* winning. How could you let him down by *cheating?*" Mellisa knew her words were cruel, but she was angry.

He took the insult without flinching. "Touché, Sis. The deal is—no one would ever suspect that I cheated. But I did. I lied to Dad and Sampson. Told them I was working on something so great no one could read it until I was finished. Truth is, I wrote nothing until the night before it was due."

The memory came back to Mellisa. "You stayed up here that night. I thought you'd fallen asleep."

"No, I pulled an all-nighter. Wrote the poems and stories for the almighty Tabor committee. For Dad and Mr. Sampson." He gestured at the bookshelves. "I figured if I stole words verbatim from successful but dead obscure authors, I might be able to fool everybody."

Mellisa couldn't believe what she was hearing. "And?"

He shrugged. "Well, it worked. Nobody noticed."

"Yet," Mellisa added.

Andy shoved the reference book back into place on the shelf. "You're right. I'd live in fear that someday I'd be exposed."

He slumped into a chair. "I guess you could also call me a coward. Look what Dad did when he was my age. Turned down his father's money and left home just to be true to his own beliefs. And me? I caved."

Reaching across the desk, he slammed a notebook shut to punctuate his comment. "At least Dad's choice let him sleep at night. Mine is a prison—as long as I live."

As long as I live echoed in Mellisa's head. She blocked unpleasant images from her mind's eye.

"Remember the poem Sampson loved about the girl who followed the sailor to sea?" Andy continued.

Mellisa remembered.

"I stole it from a guy named William Anthony Tyndale, who can't sue me because he's been dead for two hundred years.

"Oh, Andy, your reputation—"

"Is shot," he finished. "I thought I could go on stage, accept the award, make Sampson happy, make my dad proud, then never do this again, but . . ." With sudden anger, he shoved a stack of papers off the desk.

Mellisa watched the pages flutter to the patterned carpet. "I think it's *good* you've had an attack of conscience."

He glowered at her. "Easy for you to say. You don't have an auditorium filled with people waiting to applaud a success that isn't yours."

Mellisa glanced at her watch. The program was well underway. Mrs. Castano was probably pacing the parking lot, searching for Andy,

50

while keeping his absence a secret from Mr. Sampson, whose temper was best avoided.

Somewhere on a floor below, a phone rang. Had to be Dad. Ready to send out a search party for his kids.

Andy came to his feet. "Who answered the phone?"

"Relax, it's only Jackson." Mellisa was glad Jackson was there to catch the phone and explain things to Dad as best he could. Taking a breath, she plunged on. "Let's go."

Andy gave her an incredulous look. "Go where?"

"To school. You've got unfinished business."

Surprise and fear shadowed his face in the lamplight. "Are you crazy? I can't go on stage and pretend—"

"You're not going to."

"What do you mean?" He studied her face. "Ho, wait a minute. You want me to go up there and confess? Tell everyone I plagiarized the winning entry in the Tabor competition? Tell everyone I'm a fraud?"

By the end of the questions, he was screaming at her.

"Yes, Andrew James Meeker the fourth. You have a way with words. You'll think of something to say while we're driving."

"Words." He spat it out like a curse. "They're only words."

Opening the door, Mellisa motioned for him to follow.

"Hey, wait!" Andy yanked her away from the stairwell. "Five minutes ago, I was about jump off the damn ledge. If you hadn't shown up when you did, I'd . . . I'd . . ."

"Still be sitting there." Remembering Andy's tie, Mellisa rescued it from the desk and wrapped it around his neck, tucking it beneath his collar. He stood quietly, acting defeated, letting her smooth his hair and fumble with the tie. "I know you too well. You would *not* end your life just to save face."

A tear escaped from the corner of his eye. He slashed at his cheek with one hand, acting annoyed that emotions would betray him. "So you think I don't have enough guts to let go of the ledge?"

Not answering, she flubbed the knot on his tie for the third time. Pushing her hands away, he tied it himself.

"Facing everyone at school will require all the guts you can muster."

Mellisa was suddenly aware of Jackson shuffling in the stairwell. How long had he been listening?

Andy turned away, hugging himself the way he used to when he was little and something had scared him. "I can't do it, Mell. I can't face them."

She touched his shoulder. "Yes, you can. You've been on that stage before, Mr. Debate Captain. You know how to win an audience over with words."

He scoffed. "This is different. What words do I offer tonight? How I've let Whitman down? Why I can't accept the honor?"

She held his gaze for a long moment. "Couldn't have said it better myself."

He pointed a finger at her. "I'll get even for this, little sister."

He said it in jest, but she knew he meant it. "Touché," she answered.

The auditorium was dark when they arrived. Teresa Fuji was playing a flute solo. Teresa always played flute solos, but Mellisa didn't remember her being on tonight's program. Some rearranging must have been done to stall for the belated arrival of one of the award recipients.

Mrs. Castano, stationed in the hall, waved the instant she spotted them, then flew to the stage door to alert Mr. Sampson.

"Jackson and I will sit in back," Andy whispered. "Tell Dad we're here."

Great. I get to walk down the aisle while someone's performing.

Keeping her eyes focused on the footlights, Mellisa hurried toward the stage. Hunching over, she scuttled to her seat.

Dad greeted her with a flurry of whispered questions.

She calmed him down, promising to explain later.

Mellisa sat stiffly, applauding for Teresa and her flute. As the lights came up, she noticed that the athletes were clutching trophies. So. The sports awards were over. Andy must be last.

Mr. Sampson strode across the stage. His furrowed brow didn't tell Mellisa anything, since his brow was always furrowed.

He harrumphed a few times into the microphone and glared at the audience like he did at every assembly. Mellisa expected him to act differently when parents were present, but he never did.

The teacher began by thanking the audience for allowing him to re-arrange the order of presentations. Then he launched into the history of the Tabor Medal, how it had been inspired by a talented student back in the seventies who went on to write for the theater and now funded the citywide award: an engraved cut-glass paperweight for the winner, plus two thousand dollars for the winning school's library.

Mr. Sampson spoke glowingly of this year's winner, making sure the audience know that *he* was Andy's lit teacher, as though taking credit for the win.

A few chuckles rippled through the crowd. Mellisa didn't think Mr. Sampson had meant for his bragging to be funny.

During the rave introduction, pride flickered on her father's face. Groaning, Mellisa squirmed in her seat. The next ten minutes promised to be excruciating.

Applause carried her brother down the aisle and onto the stage. His tie was on straight, his sports jacket buttoned, and his hair combed. He looked like the same confident brother Mellisa had seen on stage before.

Her hands began to shake in empathy. She'd die if that many people were staring at her, waiting for her to speak.

Andy waited for the applause to die down. He opened a wrinkled paper clutched in his hands and smoothed it onto the podium.

"Before I begin," he said, "I'd like to ask my sister, Mellisa Meeker, to join me up here at the podium."

His words stopped Mellisa's breath. *What's he doing!? This has nothing to do with me. He knows I can't go up there.*

Andy shaded his eyes with one hand and peered into the audience. Dad nudged her. "Hey, Mell, he wants to share his moment of glory with his sister. Go on up."

"Mellisa?" Andy spoke her name slowly, the way he said it whenever he was doing something to get even.

She knew. She knew what he was doing. Since she was making him face his biggest fear, and not taking *no* for an answer, he was making her do the same. Face her own fear. Her biggest nightmare.

The audience began to applaud—to speed things up, she figured. Suddenly Mrs. Castano was there, pulling her out of her seat. Being paralyzed, she couldn't have gotten to her feet any other way.

Andy, don't make me do this!

She gave him a desperate, pleading stare. Just hearing her name spoken into the microphone had already spun her heart out of control.

Mrs. Castano urged her toward the stairs, clutching her arm as if she sensed Mellisa was in a fight-or-flight mode.

Climbing the steps on shaky legs, she stood beside her brother, focusing on him instead of the audience. Or on all those eyes, staring at her.

Andy put one hand over the microphone and whispered, "Do I need to say, 'Touché'?"

"Shut up and give your damn speech. And don't you *dare* make me say anything."

He grinned at her. She could not grin back, yet his smile and the look in his eyes kept her knees from buckling. No, he wouldn't make her speak. She knew he wasn't trying to be cruel. He needed her here.

He needed her.

Mellisa dared a glance at the audience. She couldn't see a thing! Thank God for the blinding brightness. Made her feel that she and Andy were here alone. The thought surged calmness through her. With the calmness came the sense that things would truly be all right.

Whitman High was about to receive its biggest shock of the year. People would gossip about the Meeker boy for weeks—months maybe. But eventually they'd turn to other topics, and this night would be forgotten.

"Friends, classmates, teachers, and guests," Andy began.

Mellisa's terrified heart overflowed with pride. Andy's voice was strong, like he owned the audience. As long as she focused on him and let the hazy cloud of footlights shield her, she was *almost* okay.

"I came here tonight to accept the Tabor Medal, given for excellence in writing."

Andy paused—a beat too long. Mellisa could hear the audience shifting, uncomfortable at the extended silence.

"I am declining this prestigious award."

A collective gasp *whooshed* from the crowd.

Mellisa glanced offstage. A startled Mr. Sampson put a hand behind one ear as if he thought hadn't heard correctly.

"The body of work I turned in for consideration by the Tabor Committee was not my own," Andy continued. "I know this was absolutely wrong. I cannot stand here and give you a valid excuse. I can only say that I could not live with myself if I perpetrated this dishonest act."

Facing Mr. Sampson, he said, "Sir, I am truly sorry." Squinting beyond the footlights, he added, "Dad? I ask your forgiveness."

The silence in the auditorium was much louder than the thunderous applause had been after Andy's introduction.

Stepping back from the podium, he held out a hand to Mellisa.

She grasped his hand, pleased that he knew she'd never make it across the stage and down the steps without someone to hold onto. "You chose the perfect words," she whispered.

He shrugged, as if turning down awards was a nightly habit. Holding her hand like a lifeline, he led her off stage. Mellisa realized for the first time that the lifeline ran both directions. Her overly confident brother needed her as much as she-of-little-confidence needed him. Go figure.

Mellisa fully expected Andy to keep on going—right out the emergency exit and far away from this place.

But he didn't.

He led her back to the seats in the front row.

She tried to read her father's face, but it was a strange mixture of sadness and awe.

Rising, Dad put his arms around his son, holding him in silence.

Mellisa hung back, hating the way this private moment was being witnessed. It reminded her of Mom's funeral, how Dad had broken down in front of everyone, and how she couldn't bear to see him like that.

How she'd fled to get away from staring eyes, and how Andy had come looking for her. Hiding in a juniper grove in Alpine Park in freezing rain, they'd cried together.

For a long moment no one in the auditorium moved or spoke.

Then Mr. Sampson stepped to the microphone. Mellisa could tell he was shaken, because he wasn't scowling as usual. His expression surprised her. It was not one of disappointment, but of astonishment.

"Before I turn the program back to Principal Osaka, I'd like to say that the short speech we've just heard must have caused Andy Meeker a great deal of pain to deliver. I cannot applaud Mr. Meeker on the actions he has confessed. But I can applaud him on his honesty in stopping the lie."

Andy began to tremble. The difficult part was over. Mellisa figured his brain must have just kicked in. Dad kept one arm firmly around his son's shoulders.

"Andy," Mr. Sampson finished. "I implore you to put tonight's experience behind you. But tomorrow. Ah, tomorrow and tomorrow and tomorrow, I . . . we—the entire community of Whitman High— we expect great things from you."

No one applauded. It would have been a perfect ending, but Mellisa knew applause would let Andy off the hook too easily. His punishment wasn't over. He still had to face everyone—in the halls and on the street. That, too, would take guts.

The Meeker family sat down to wait out the closing song by the Whitman Senior Chorale. "The Long and Winding Road."

How appropriate, Mellisa thought.

Andy nudged her. His face was pale, but a spark still glinted in his eyes. "And I," he whispered, "expect great things from you, Mellisa Emily Meeker the first."

"You got it," she told him. "I'll say *anything* to make you happy. After all, they're only *words*."

She knew his response before he said it.

"Touché."

BY ANNA GROSSNICKLE HINES

Stage Fright

"Mom! Thank gawd you're finally home! I've got the absolute worst news! They picked me to be one of the speakers at graduation."

Mom's back is to me, but I see her freeze, just for an instant, before she slides the grocery bags onto the counter. She catches her purse as it slips off her shoulder and takes a breath. I'm waiting for the, "Oh, you poor baby," but she turns around and says, "Well, Angela! That's wonderful!"

And she's beaming at me! Beaming! The tired look she had on her face when she came through the door suddenly gone.

"But, Mom . . ." This is *not* what I expected! Wonderful? Did she really say wonderful?

She hurries over to gather me in for one of her great hugs. "Congratulations! That's terrific news!"

But, Mom . . ." I pull back to look at her. This can't be *my* mother!

Have I been transported into some alternate universe? Where's my sympathetic understanding? Has she forgotten about my problem?

"You know what this means," I say. "Grandma and Grandpa are coming all the way from Arizona, and . . ." I blink, but can't stop the waterworks. "It's my only ninth grade graduation. I don't want to miss it."

Mom puts a hand under my chin and lifts my face. "You won't miss it. You'll give a wonderful speech, and you'll be just fine." She wipes a tear off my cheek and kisses the wet spot. "You'll be fine." She smiles and nods, then gives me one more squeeze before turning back to the grocery bag.

"But what about 'The Ugly Duckling' and the Christmas angel and . . . and the daffodil? What about the daffodil, Mom? That wasn't the flu all those times, you know! What if . . . ?"

Mom interrupts, using her end-of-discussion voice. "That was a long time ago. You were too little to manage. This is now. This is different. You'll be just fine." She hands me a head of lettuce. "Here. Make a salad."

I take the lettuce and stand there with my mouth hanging open. My poor mother is out of her mind. She must have been working even harder than I thought. I stare as she bustles around, putting the rest of the groceries away, then folds the bag and slips it in the space between the wall and the refrigerator.

I try again. "But I'm the one who gets the *backstage* jobs, remember?" There's a very good reason that for every program after second grade I got to be the Person in Charge of Opening and Closing the Door or the One Who Hands Out the Tambourines at the Last Minute. I never made it through one single performance on stage. Not even the Fly-Up Ceremony for my Brownie Troop when all I had to do was walk across the bridge to get my wings and become a real

Girl Scout. The thought of all those people watching sent me off to the toilet, where I had a little private ceremony of my own.

Mom knows all that very well, but still all she says is, "You'll be fine." Then off she goes down the hall calling, "Don't forget to put a tomato in that salad, and let's use French dressing tonight. I'll be back as soon as I get out of these work clothes."

My mother is glad I've been chosen! She's got to be out of her mind. What is she thinking? I rip the lettuce to shreds as my thoughts rage. This isn't some stupid grammar school Christmas program. This is graduation. I chop the bloody tomato to bits. This is important, and she won't even listen to me.

I don't even try to talk at dinner. Not much point anyway. My sister Julie is going on and on to Mom about some girl she's mad at because she told some other girl something that this girl told Julie not to tell anybody but Julie told the first girl or something like that. Like Julie really has a problem. Julie who comes along three years after the Throw-up Queen and stars in every program her class puts on.

Later, when Mom comes in to tell me she's going to bed, I'm doing my homework. At least I'm staring at the page. Not too much is getting in my head, because my feelings are so jumbled up. I don't look at her. She comes over and rubs my shoulders.

"You really can do this, Angela," she says. "You just have to believe you can."

"You don't understand," I say. How come all of a sudden she's expecting me to be cool and calm like her? Like Julie?

In first grade when I was supposed to read 'The Ugly Duckling' while the other kids acted it out, they thought I had the flu and got Kevin Manabe to take my place at the last minute. It happened again in second grade when I was supposed to be a Christmas angel, so Mom figured out it was stage fright, and that spring when I was picked to be one of the daffodils she encouraged me to try to get through it. "What if I throw up?" I said. "Just run to the bathroom," she'd told me. "Run real quick." I'd tried, but it hadn't worked.

Doesn't she remember what a disaster that had been? Apparently not.

"I do understand," she says and lets out a big sigh. "More than you know."

I look at her. "Couldn't you just call . . . ?"

Before I even get the question out, she's shaking her head. "No. Because you can do it. You really will be fine." She kisses the top of my head, says good night and leaves me sitting there.

I scrap the homework and crawl into bed, but it takes me a long time to get to sleep. My mom was wrong to tell me I could be a good daffodil, and she's wrong now. I can't do that speech. No way. I thump my pillow. She doesn't understand at all. Not at all. I'm just going to have to handle the problem myself.

The next day, I go straight to Ms. Murphy, English teacher extraordinaire and adviser for our class. I know she'll try to talk me out of resigning as class speaker, but I'll be tough. I'll stand my ground. I just have to get to her while nobody else is around. I ease her door open, hoping to get a feel for her mood before I present my case, but one glance at me and she snaps out, "Speech done?"

I shake my head. She glares. It's not a mean glare. It's one she does a lot, with the corners of her mouth tucked back to keep from smiling. It means she's serious, but not mad or anything. I gulp. My stomach's working my breakfast over pretty good.

"That's what I wanted to talk to you about," I say.

"Yyyeeeessss?" She peers at me over the top of her glasses.

"I can't do it. I'm going to be sick." Any minute now, I think.

"You're planning ahead to be sick?" she says. "Are you going to be coming down with malaria or hepatitis, or will it be some new disease they haven't invented yet?" She's still peering, with her head cocked to the side now.

Very amusing, Ms. Murphy! I look at the floor. "Every time I have to go on stage I get sick."

"You and a few hundred thousand other people," Ms. Murphy says.

"No, I mean really sick. In second grade when I was a daffodil I threw up all over the crocuses."

"That must have been interesting."

Interesting! I tell her about the worst experience of my life and she says it must have been interesting! There I was with my daffodil costume sticking out like a crown all around my face, and my stomach trying to leap out of my throat. "Run for the bathroom," Mom had said, so I pushed my way through the bluebells and tulips, and I was right out in front of everybody when I couldn't hold back another millisecond. Vomit spewed everywhere. The spring peepers mostly leaped out of the way, but the crocuses were all crouched down, and they couldn't do anything but scream. Interesting? Yeah, right, Ms. Murphy.

I look up at her. She's trying not to smile. Smile! How can she! But suddenly, in spite of myself, I'm trying not to smile, too, and we both let out little chuckles.

"Well," I say, feeling relieved. "Now you know you should get Janice to be the speaker instead of me." I know it'll be Janice because she has the next highest GPA after me and Manuelo Perez, who is the other speaker.

"I don't know any such thing," Ms. Murphy says.

"But . . ."

She gets up and puts an arm around my shoulders and starts slowly walking me to the door. "Angela, my dear, nobody ever died of stage fright."

"There's a first time for everything," I warn her.

62

"Write your speech!" she says.

So that night I write my speech.

On Saturday, Mom takes me shopping for my graduation dress. I don't see much point, since I'll only be wearing it in the bathroom. Mom's bubbling over with enthusiasm, showing me this and showing me that. I'm still mad at her for not understanding me. "What difference does it make?" I say, when she shoves about the seventeenth dress in my face. "You know I'm not going to get to wear it anyway. I'm not Julie, you know!"

"Thank goodness!" Mom says. "One of Julie is enough! And one of you is enough, too! Now don't be so melodramatic. Do you know that lots of famous actors throw up before every performance? You'll just have to get your timing right. Now go and try this dress."

I snatch it and go into the dressing room, muttering, "Get my timing right." Yeah, sure. Like *when* I puke all over the stage is going to make any difference. Do I do it before the speeches or after?

But that dress—I slip it over my head and catch a glimpse of myself in the mirror. That dress fits me as if it's specially made, nipping in at my waist princess style and flowing down almost to my ankles. It makes all my best features show up and the worst ones go into hiding. It's *my* dress. I go out to show Mom, and she sees it, too.

"Oh!" she says. "Oh, Angela. It's perfect!" She smoothes it over my shoulders, steps back for another look, and smiles. "Perfect!"

Even some of the other people in the shop are smiling at me and saying how good I look.

Mom checks the price tag and I see her kind of gulp. I reach for it, but she pushes my hand away. "Never mind about that," she says. "It's the right dress."

And I'm selfish enough to be glad. I'm thinking maybe in a dress like that I just might be able to get through that speech.

63

Manuelo and I rehearse a couple of times that next week. It's just the two of us with Ms. Murphy, so it's not so bad. But then we start rehearsing with the whole class. Ms. Murphy calls Manny and me up onto the stage to make sure our chairs are in the right place. I tell her maybe she should arrange to have a toilet next to the podium.

"Very funny," she says, but Manny gets a good chuckle out of it.

"You nervous?" he says.

"Only terrified," I say. "Aren't you?"

"No sweat," he says. Then he pulls a handkerchief out of his pocket and wipes the drops off his forehead. He grins, and I grin back. He's probably not going to be all that bad looking, when he grows about ten more inches.

Ms. Murphy shows me where she's put a trash can right behind the curtain. "Not that you're going to need it, silly girl."

Silly girl, yourself, I think. Clearly, she does not understand the seriousness of the situation, any more than my mother does.

At first everybody keeps screwing up the march, so we don't get to the speeches, which is okay by me. Finally Mr. Flint says we're going straight through no matter what. Oh, joy! As Manny gives his speech I'm telling myself it won't be so bad, not so different from giving a report in front of a class. Right! Only five times as many kids! I wish my friend Nina were out there. We always got each other through oral reports by pretending we were just talking to each other, but her cruel and inhumane parents moved her away over Christmas vacation, just five months before graduation.

I look for some other face I might talk to. Sherri Crandall is rolling her eyes. Janice looks like she's dying for me. Dying to be in my place, more likely. I wish she was. I'm up. I get through the speech, mostly looking right over the heads to the back wall, trying to pretend it's all empty chairs out there. We go through the whole thing again, then again. By the time we're through everybody's so bored with rehears-

64

ing that the chairs might as well be empty for all the attention being paid. But the real audience is still to come.

Grandma and Grandpa arrive from Arizona and fuss all over me. They fuss over Julie some, too, but mostly me. Grandma keeps saying, "Valedictorian! Imagine that! Our little Angela, valedictorian! We're just so proud! So proud!" Grandpa doesn't say much, just winks at me when he sees Grandma is making me feel embarrassed, but his eyes say the same as her chattering.

"It reminds me of your mother when she was valedictorian," Grandma says.

"Mom was valedictorian?" I say. This is news to me.

"We don't need to talk about that," Mom says.

"Talk about what?" I say. "What happened?"

"Nothing," Mom says. "I was fine." She looks at Grandma.

Grandma looks at me. "That's right, dear. She was just fine and you will be, too."

I can hardly eat any supper. I say I don't want anything, but Mom insists a piece of toast and a little tea are a good idea. My hair comes out decent, and I manage to not smear mascara all over my face even though my hands are shaking. The earrings Grandma and Grandpa gave me look great with the dress, which is almost as magic as the first time, in spite of the fact that I've been trying it on every day after school. Then Mom pops up with a corsage as the finishing touch. I've never felt so elegant in my life. Even Julie says I look good, and by the way she keeps sneaking peeks at me out of the corner of her eye, like she's trying to figure out how such a miracle could happen, I can tell she really thinks so.

Grandma pats my cheek and coos, "Oh, sweet Angela. So much like your mother."

Me? Like my mother? My calm, cool, collected mother? I don't think so!

65

My stomach is pretty jumpy, but so far everything is going fine. Then, just as we're about to go out the door, I get this feeling in my nose, and before I realize what it is, blood gushes out all over the front of my white dress. I wail and pinch, tipping my head back. Grandma gasps. Julie shrieks. Even Grandpa looks worried. Mom springs into action. She grabs a washcloth, sticks it under the faucet, and starts shooing the rest of them out of the house.

"Go on," she says. "We'll take two cars. You go on and save me a seat. We'll be right there. Everything is going to be fine."

Grandpa takes over from there and whooshes Grandma and Julie out the door, with Grandma still chattering. "Can't I do something to help?" and Julie wailing, "Oh, your dress! It's gross!"

It is gross, but it's also polyester. Mom has one washcloth under my nose and is carefully sponging at the bloody blotches with another, all the time talking calmly. "It's going to be fine. We'll just clean this up and get the bleeding stopped. There's plenty of time. You're going to be just fine."

Now I know for sure my poor mother has totally lost her mind. It had looked that way when she first thought my being chosen to speak was wonderful news, but this is really pushing it. My nose is gushing like a wounded "Old Faithful," my dress is ruined, the ceremony is minutes away, and my mother is still telling me it's going to be fine. I'm not in a position to argue. I'm too busy dealing with the nose. By the time the bleeding stops, every spot on the front of my dress is gone. Mom the miracle worker. Except for my nose being all red from the pinching and wiping, and the fact that my stomach is writhing worse than ever, I'm as good as new.

Mom smiles. "Well, we handled that, didn't we? I told you it would be fine." But just in case it's not, she gives me a clean washcloth before whisking me into the car. When we get to school, Mom hustles me to the gym, where the kids are already lining up, dashes into the girls' bathroom, and comes out to trade my washcloth for a smaller, more discreet, damp paper towel, then hurries off to her seat. She only looks back once, a little nervously, I think, but when she sees me looking at her, she smiles, gives me one last wave, and goes on.

Ms. Murphy is running about ten directions at once trying to get everybody to line up and behave. She stops and puts a hand on my shoulder. "So how are the butterflies?"

"Butterflies nothing," I tell her. "I've got june bugs. Big ones!" She flaps her hand at me and goes off, leaving me staring at the back of Donald Henderson's head. He has a big old pimple on his neck. I wonder if I have any popping out on my face. I didn't have any signs when I left home, but you never know. They always show up at the worst times. I tell myself to stop thinking about that, but then I start thinking about the paper towel in my hand, wondering how much good it's going to do if it's my stomach instead of my nose that decides to spew next.

The music starts. "You'll be fine," I repeat to myself. "You'll be fine." If only I could believe it. *Daaa da da daa daaa daaa.* I put one foot in front of the other, keep my spacing all the way down the aisle, past the audience, past the seats where my classmates are filing in, across the front of the auditorium, up the steps, and onto the stage to take my place next to Manuelo. My knees are jumping up and down like a flickering picture on the television. "Pomp and Circumstance" vibrato. *D-a-a-a d-a d-a d-a-a d-a-a-a d-a-a-a.*

I stare straight ahead into that sea of faces, and my head starts to spin. "Just breathe," I say to myself. "Just breathe. You're going to be fine." Mom is out there someplace, with Grandpa and Grandma and Julie. I partly want to find them and partly don't. I try keeping my eyes on my classmates, counting them as they file into the rows, wishing my name was Zupko instead of Houston. It would have been better to be the last one in. I watch Janice as she comes down the aisle and walks across. That's when I see where my family is. Julie waves, dumb kid. I don't let myself look at any of their faces. *Daaa da da daa daaa daaa.* Finally everyone is in place.

Mr. Flint goes to the mike and calls for us to remain standing for the Pledge of Allegiance. Then he does a little welcome thing. We get to sit down for that, and I'm glad because I'm about to keel over. Mr. Flint thanks all the families for coming and goes on for a while telling the parents that if it weren't for their support, our success wouldn't be possible, and I'm thinking, my Mom might have been a little more supportive and told them about me, so I wouldn't be sitting up here with hundreds of eyes watching to see if I scratch myself or remember to keep my legs together, which I don't and do. Don't scratch and do keep my legs together, and also keep my hands folded in my lap, sitting stiff and straight as a statue. None of those hundreds of watching eyes, except the eight that are related to me, have any clue that scratching or not keeping my legs together are nothing compared to what I'm afraid is going to happen.

At least Manny has to speak first. I know his speech almost as well as I know my own, and the closer he gets to the end of it, the tenser I get. The paper towel in my hand is squeezed so tight it's almost a toothpick.

I hear Mom's voice in my head. "You'll be fine." Easy for her to say. *Oh, Mom, why didn't you get me out of this? Why didn't you save me?* Suddenly I want to see her face. Manny is almost finished. It's almost time for my speech. I need to see my mother. I look. She's looking back at me. She gives a little nod.

Manny is finished. Mr. Flint is introducing me.

Oh, please, Mom, I can't!

"You can," her eyes say. "You'll be fine."

I stand up and walk to the mike, my eyes locked on my mother's face, the only face in a vast sea of shapes and colors. I take a breath.

68

"We are on a journey," I begin. I speak for my mother. I keep going, one sentence after the other. Other faces start coming into focus, listening faces, smiling faces. My grandma's face. She dabs at her eyes with a tissue. Grandpa's face, beaming pride. Even Julie looks proud of me. My knees shake and the june bugs boogie, but I'm not paying attention to that anymore. I give my whole speech, looking back at Mom as I say my last words. Everyone starts clapping, and suddenly my chest fills with air. Swells up like a balloon.

I've done it! I get back to my chair, sit down, and manage to hold out for the rest of the ceremony, in spite of the fact that the june bugs are doing the Hallelujah Chorus. Please, just let me make it until the end of the program. Don't let me blow it now. But as soon as the last kid has her diploma and the last words of congratulations to the class are spoken, I jump up and slip behind the curtain. My stomach heaves. The trash can! It's gone! Quickly, I head for the restroom, practically gagging every step of the way. I rush into a stall, lean over the toilet and let it go. Tea and toast revisited.

Somebody comes in behind me. I reach back to push the door of the stall closed. How embarrassing! But at least I'm not on stage. One last heave and I stand up to catch my breath. That's when I hear a familiar sound in the next stall, and it's not made by anybody sitting down. Poor girl, and she hadn't even had to give a speech. I go to the sink, rinse my mouth, and wipe it with a paper towel. The door of the other stall opens and in the mirror I see . . .

"Mom!"

Her white face smiles at me. "I told you," she says, "timing is everything."

About Russell

"Give me a number. Any positive number!" my brother Russell said, hot on the enthusiasm of his latest discovery. It had something to do with being able to calculate square roots in a way other than using the standard method.

My sister, brother, and I were all talented in some area. I read early and spontaneously, my sister Rosalind was a gifted artist, and my brother Russell loved science and math. Close in age, we were each other's friends, audiences, and co-conspirators—although this did not stop us from occasionally ganging up, two against one. For the most part, we were each other's allies and listened to each other's ideas and dreams.

"MIT here I come," Russell said.

Mommy, who was listening from the living room said, "That ain't nothing."

Rosalind and I translated Mommy's remark in the three ways she meant it: 1) "Square roots won't put beans on the table," 2) "No one's going to let black boys discover nothing else but basketball," and 3) "If you're so smart, why can't you score over eighty in school?"

Russell gave a muffled but nervous laugh that went under his breath and out through his nose. Then Rosalind and I giggled too, mainly so he wouldn't be laughing alone.

Russell still believed he had something. Anxious to prove Mommy wrong, he brought his discovery to Mr. Hershkowitz, his math teacher, who was both impressed and excited that one of his students thought about math beyond doing the homework. This was understandable. Russell and I attended Junior High School 192 in Hollis, New York, a school that in the early seventies was noted for drug trafficking, gang infestation, and a bloody playground murder.

Envisioning the paths where Russell's discovery could lead him, Rosalind and I began grooming him for interviews with the local news and math journals. In our minds, Russell's future was bright and without limitation, starting with a full scholarship to MIT or Northwestern.

We waited to hear further developments. After weeks of researching Russell's square root formula, Mr. Hershkowitz found that some graduate student had written a paper about it. Mr. Hershkowitz still offered encouragement to Russell and sent away for this paper so Russell could see how mathematicians presented ideas. I remember him reading it, giving that low laugh of his in intervals as he read.

"Hey Russell, look at it this way," Rosalind said. "It took a Ph.D. to discover what you found on your own in the eighth grade."

Mommy said, "I 'bout figured it was nothing."

This didn't stop Russell from making discoveries. I recall one night in July Rosalind and I couldn't sleep in our room, which had neither a fan nor air conditioning. We were baking, so we opened our window for fresh air even though it meant being eaten by mosquitoes nesting in the sweet pine two feet from the window. The air cooled the room and we finally drifted off to sleep some time after one o'clock. It was a short sleep, for at two-thirty-seven A.M. the lights switched on, framing Russell's lanky figure in the doorway.

"Guess what?" He exclaimed, waiting for our rejoinder.

We groaned.

"I can calculate the distance the earth will spin off its axis by the year 2000!"

Our pillows went flying in the doorway before he could give details.

By my freshman year in high school our parents had finally separated, much to our relief. They had been fighting nonstop during the three years that Daddy had been home from Vietnam. They argued day in and day out. Anything from Rosalind mentioning art school to Daddy wanting Russell to wash his car provoked an argument. The house was always in a state of war, and we heard every word.

Rosalind and I seemed to handle their fighting as best we could, however, Russell was always affected. On one hand, he wanted to protect Mommy—although Mommy always got the best of Daddy. On the other hand, Russell was angry at her too.

Their separation was a blessing. Rosalind, Russell, and I hated going on welfare but we preferred the relative peace in our home to the battleground. Russell seemed to benefit most of all, coming into his own in high school. For one thing, Mommy didn't fuss too much when he got a part-time job through the Youth Corps, and her objections to his joining the track team at school were clearly ceremonial.

Before our eyes, Russell became a different person. His teammates nicknamed him Cobra because his head weaved from side to side as he climbed uphill in his cross-country runs. *A nickname! Actual friends!* Rosalind and I thought. We were thrilled that Russell had come out of his shell. Every night following practice he'd entertain us with hilarious stories of Rico, Francois, E-Train, and Vernon, imitating their put-downs, gestures, and running styles. He had never been so animated. The following year he was made co-captain of the team and helped coach the girls' track team.

Things were going well. One morning in his senior year there was a knock at the door at about 6:45 A.M. From our bedroom, Rosalind and I glued our Afroed heads to the window to get a glimpse of the caller. I was sure the woman was a friend of Rosalind's from college. Rosalind was sure the caller was a friend of Mommy's because she was too "grown" to be one of her friends.

At a closer look, we could see that the woman was a girl with school books, and that she had come asking for our brother Russell.

The two of us ran to the top of the stairs to peer down at the doorway where Mommy stood, then back to the window to see the girl. We slapped Russell on the back as he made it downstairs.

From the top of the stairs we saw our mother, speechless and powerless, as her son brushed past her to greet Sherri. It was a big event. A girl had come knocking on the door for our brother. She stood there, as bold as day, letting Mommy know she was there for her son. Russell came downstairs and the two walked off. He seemed to have an entire conversation for her and she was interested. *Gasp! They were holding hands!*

Rosalind and I were ecstatic. It was so important to us, this validation that our brother was normal. Russell had developed a stubbornness over the years, a wall between himself and other people. Even when we were much younger, living in California, he would go out of his way to alienate our friends for no particular reason. He knocked over game boards or just plain old quit when things weren't going his way.

I recall playing the greatest kickball game ever, back in Seaside, Cal-

73

ifornia, with five on each team, the score tied, and the right to shout, "We won!" at stake. The bases were loaded and Rosalind, the tie-breaker, stood at the plate, ready to kick one down Vallejo Street. Russell hurled the ball to the plate. Rosalind trotted to meet the pitch then kicked it hard but low, straight into Russell's hands. With the ball still in his hands, Russell calmly left the playing field, walked to our house, and went inside. No one could believe it. The greatest kickball game ever and Russell ended it without an explanation.

He couldn't be moved. Names, no matter how harshly thrown, rolled right off his back—or it seemed that way. Our pleas always went unanswered. Bribes were considered but were ultimately dismissed. Russell's strongest weapon was his "NO" and he used it often. I think it came from his always being constantly pulled between Mommy, who wanted an obedient son, and Daddy, who wanted a platoon leader. In his way Russell held his ground, but from some angry, inarticulate place, deep within himself. Rosalind and I didn't know that his self-erected wall was how he protected himself. We just thought he was being a pain in the butt.

When he wasn't being obstinate, he was the opposite, sharing what he knew, especially with me, his little sister. In fact, he taught me to play chess, back when the Bobby Fischer–Boris Spassky matches were being televised. I'm sure he taught me to play only to have a target to punish. I was just so pleased my brother would give me the time of day. I'd make my sheepish moves, and he'd swoop down and take my pieces as quickly as my hand retracted from them. Sometimes he'd let me go along advancing my pieces down the board, only to find myself in an irrevocable predicament. These games were always humiliating for me, but Russell enjoyed them.

Eventually I had enough of humiliation and began playing chess with the guys next door. They smoked a lot of reefer and were just learning the game, so I won most of these matches. As I played the guys next door, I developed a sense of rhythm and strategy for the game, and chess became fun.

One Saturday evening in August, just before I went away to college, my brother and I sat down to play a game of chess. I don't remember any of the particulars, just that I said "checkmate" about twenty minutes after we began. He just grinned, looked down at the board, and said, "hmm," the way he did when he found a flaw in one of his discoveries.

I was amazed. Not so much that I had won, but that he let my pieces stand in victory on the board. Although he had matured since his days of knocking the pieces off the board, I at least expected him to put the chess set away.

I was too proud of my victory to linger on my brother's good sportsmanship. Instead I marveled at my black chessmen dominating white territory. I took inventory of his captured pieces, relishing the playback of each seizure. This was more than a game to me. It was a trophy, because I had beaten my brother.

The pieces stood on the table, even as I left home to go off to college. Strangely enough, the board remained intact when I came home that Thanksgiving, and for winter break as well. When I brought my things home the following summer, I looked at the table and saw that my queen, rook, and bishop still cornered his lone king. In my mind, I explained the chessboard as a shrine maintained by our mother. She needed to remember that she had children who once played games in her house.

We were all grown and out of the house, except for Russell. Rosalind had an apartment and went to LaGuardia Community College for accounting. (Mommy picked out her major.)

Russell didn't get into MIT, but we'd figured he wouldn't, since his grades were average. He was, however, accepted into Penn State on a partial track scholarship, but the tuition and room and board were still too expensive. Besides, Mommy didn't want him to attend college out of state. Instead Russell went to New York Technology at Old Westbury. This was perfect, because both our schools were on Long Island. Russell commuted back and forth and would visit me in my dorm at Hofstra.

All the while that we were growing up, he always called me Rita or Squirt or Sloppy Joe. Now that I was a woman, he called me "Little Sister." Feeling somewhat lost in my new environment, I didn't mind too much. Besides, my big brother helped me paint my dorm room, gave me twenty dollars, and brought me a television set from home.

Eager to impress him, I told him of my chess exploits—how I joined the chess team and never went to the dining hall without my magnetic chess set. He seemed only mildly interested.

He then told me about New York Tech and his course load. College math and science were different from everything he had ever read—and he had read many books. "I like physics," he said optimistically. He laughed nervously and added, "Now if I could only pass those exams."

At the end of his sophomore year, Russell dropped out of New York Tech. We never really talked about it.

After New York Tech, he found work as a groundsman at Rochdale Village, a large co-op not far from our house. He'd run five miles in the morning, then read in the evenings when he came home from work.

Again, my brother was changing, but I couldn't really see it. I was thirty miles away, wrapped up in school. Rosalind, who wasn't too far from home, noticed changes in Russell's behavior. Things like his "yes" "no" answers. That he ate mostly peanut-butter cookies and Argo starch—which is what Black people used to eat to lighten their skin. Mommy used to give us starch to eat as children, but we had outgrown the taste for it. For whatever reason, Russell was eating starch again. His mouth was always white.

After a year, Russell was laid off from Rochdale. He found work as a security guard, but these jobs never lasted.

By my junior year I lived on campus all year round. Between sorority life, political activism, boyfriends, and modern dance I couldn't stop moving. I came home for brief visits, but these visits were too awkward without Rosalind. The house was profoundly still. Mommy stayed in her room. Russell didn't talk, let alone look at me. The chess set was still standing there, pieces and all!

Rico, one of his track buddies from high school, told me he used to see Russell walking out toward the airport every morning. He'd call and call after him, "Cobra! Hey, Cobra-man!" but Russell didn't recognize Rico and would keep on walking.

Mommy wasn't even approachable on the subject of her son and Daddy would say, "What that boy needs is a woman." I once made the suggestion that Russell be diagnosed for mental illness and got what I expected: "Take one psychology class and you know everything. You need to go on back to college. . . ."

Russell's problems were hard to ignore. He now had medical concerns, which were hard to ascertain, since he wouldn't talk. Huge boils covered his skin and he was always in pain.

Rosalind and I finally ganged up on Mommy to get her to take him to a doctor. She finally relented some of her control and took Russell to the clinic to get his boils lanced. The lancing was all that was done, and no other areas of Russell's condition were looked into.

Russell took the sanitation test several times and scored well, but they never called him for training or work. Daddy, who worked in real estate, got Russell odd jobs cleaning houses newly listed on the market, but the work wasn't steady. Always broke and without a routine, Russell became depressed.

All of Russell's prospects were far from his grasp, physically and mentally. He stopped running. Ideas did not occur to him as far as we knew. Reading was replaced by watching sci-fi TV shows. Further and further Russell slipped away, unable to make eye contact or hold a conversation. When he did speak, it was in a monotone, his eyes fixed elsewhere. Some ten years later when he came to my home for a visit, I realized he was talking to himself.

Unemployable by most standards, he took to collecting soda bottles and redeeming them for a nickel a piece. At first Rosalind and I were embarrassed. Our brother was going through peoples' garbage cans! But Rosalind put things in perspective. He never asked us for anything, nor did he go about begging other people for money. He just did whatever he could, quietly, on his own.

When I see others making strides in science and technology I tell myself, "Russell could have thought of that." I have a hard time accepting that that was Russell a long time ago.

When I talk about my brother, my well-meaning friends say, "You have to do something. Get him a job. Get him some psychiatric help." They don't understand. In spite of his illness, he has always maintained his "NO." A grown man, Russell simply will not do what he doesn't want to.

Looking back I wish I could say there were telltale signs that Russell would suffer from mental illness, but there were no incidents or episodes to point to throughout our childhood. Symptoms of his illness, his social withdrawal and talking to himself, came on gradually in his adulthood and were difficult for us to identify.

Openly discussing Russell's illness and seeking help and information would be ideal, but it is not likely to happen within my family. Perhaps it is a function of our African-American working poor background, but we're simply not talkers. My sister and I talk more about Russell's poor diet and taking steps to encourage him to eat better than about his mental health. I'm the only family member who uses the term "mental illness" regarding Russell.

Through all of my struggling to come to terms with my brother's condition, my family simply accepts him as is. Part of this is woven into our background. If we complained about indiscernible ailments as children, Mommy would say, "Don't go looking for trouble, because it will find you."

I still miss my brother.

I was out one day with my daughters shopping for groceries. It wasn't any day. It was my fortieth birthday. We turned the corner to walk down our block when Stephanie, my youngest daughter, said, "There's Uncle Russell!" He was at the garbage dump of a nearby apartment building rummaging for bottles. He looked up in time as we crossed toward him and said, "Happy birthday little sister."

I smiled and said, "Hey Russell."

BY RICHARD PECK

Waiting for Sebastian

Oh how I love the evening. Long summer evenings when the shadows of the trees creep in silent shapes across the lawn until they merge with night. I watch from this high window, framed by the old curtains held back by silk cords. I toy with the cords and watch the world dim.

When I was very small, too small to climb up on this window seat, I didn't like being put to bed when the window was still bright with summer light. I fought sleep and woke again to velvet dusk, hearing the sounds of the house beneath my cot. Only a cot then for my infant self—not like the proper grown-up bed in the room now.

The whole house and I listened to the parties Mama and Papa gave, the crystal sounds of the dinner table floating up the flights of stairs. The bark of the men's laughter and the rising scent of their cigars, after the silken sound of the ladies retiring. I love summer evenings because they take their time, dangling the dark before you.

But winter evenings warm my heart. I don't feel the cold. I watch from this window as the sun drops like a blazing penny through the bare branches, and darkness comes like a surprise.

It's winter now, the shortest day, and the sun is hurrying into the earth. This is the evening I wait for all through the year. I am curled in the window seat at the top of the house with the cat alert in my lap. This cat is a tortoiseshell, up from the barn and quite wild, but she likes me. She gazes up, perplexed and admiring. Nanny used to say that I, too, had been born in a barn, when I was smaller and naughtier. "Born in a barn," when I forgot to close the door behind me or grew tiresome in the bath.

From here the cat and I can see right to the end of the drive, now the leaves have fallen. Even the house around us waits. The statues in the lawn turn all their strange faces to the distant point where the drive meets the road. We all wait, breathless. Nothing trembles but my heart.

We get very little snow here, but in winter we are apt to get gales. They whip off the sea and cry in the attics and bend the trees double. This old window clatters in its frame, and the curtains billow, and the cord coils. Then the next morning the sky is scoured clean, and the gardener—Abel or whatever he is called—is out dragging the branches and lifting the twigs.

But this evening is as still as a painting. This is the evening when my brother will be brought up from the station, home from school. The world waits for the car to turn in at the foot of the drive.

My brother Sebastian is coming for his Christmas holidays, and I won't breathe or smile till he is here and this house is ringing with him. My brother Sebbie is coming home. But no. Wait. He says that

Sebbie is a nursery name, and now that he is at school it would be a great crime if any of his friends knew. He is Sebastian now, and even Mama must call him by that name, when she remembers. My name is Charlotte, and I think I will keep it.

When my brother first went away to school, they thought I was too young to mind. How wrong they were, how very wrong. This house is always as empty as my heart when Sebastian isn't here, though it is full of people coming and going. Sebastian went away to school at seven. Boys do.

As Papa says, "Nothing good happens at home to a boy past the age of seven." Of course he is right. At seven boys need to go live with each other in large, drafty brick places where they learn Latin verbs and tell one another terrifying tales. They eat cold cabbage and mashed potato with the eyes left in. And they are beaten when they are bad, which teaches them to be careful.

There are schools for girls to go away to, but Papa wouldn't hear of it. They play field hockey at such places, and it ruins their complexions and thickens their ankles. Papa says so. In the village, there is a school where boys and girls go together, but Mama put her foot down. "When you are married, Charlotte, you will see quite enough of the opposite sex," Mama said. "I have."

So I learn at home. After Nanny retired to a cottage, a lady came to teach me German. She wore ribbed stockings and liked country walks, but she grew homesick for her Alpine valley. The vast front of her frock was awash with her tears, and she went away. (*Auf Wiedersehen, Fräulein.*)

After her, a lady came to teach me French. She was very pretty, and the scent of a rose garden followed where she went. She had vivid red lips, though she didn't paint them. Governesses mustn't. Because Nanny was gone by then, I forgot to close the door behind me. I saw Papa kissing the French governess. She didn't mind, so I wasn't worried, but I knew it was a secret. And so I told nobody but Mama. Soon after, on the very next day, that governess left too. (*Au revoir, Mademoiselle.*)

Now I am quite on my own. But wait. Are those the headlamps of a car just turning up the drive? My forehead would be freezing, pressed against this frosty pane, if I felt the cold. Yes, the car that brings people from the station is coming up the drive. And I smile—too soon, but I can't help myself. The car takes forever, but now it's turning in the circle of gravel before the house. I peer down over the cat's ears to see—

But no. I know already it isn't Sebastian, because he always bursts out of the back door before the car rolls to a stop. Sebastian with his necktie jerked round under his ear and his scarf in the school colors flying and his socks collapsing over his shoetops. . . .

Unless, of course, it is Sebastian—later. I turn away, hoping not to see him climb manlike out of the car, unfolding his great legs and planting his snub-nosed boots on the ground. Sebastian grown and firm-chinned under his braided cap, reaching back into the car for his kit. This is not the Sebastian I pine for through the long year.

I make myself look, and it is neither of the Sebastians, nor anyone like them. It's other people, the nameless sort who come to stay and then go away. You can tell by their odd clothes and odd ways that they are foreign. Not proper visitors at all, and I can't think why Papa allows them. Perhaps we are poor now, and they pay to come here. I've thought of that. I've thought we might be poor, and Mama and Papa don't want me to know—a secret to keep me from worrying. After all, what would a family be without secrets? We would be like strangers meeting in the train, telling one another everything about ourselves.

Yes, I suppose we must be poor now. I can't think when I last saw Mama ride, and I believe she has given up her horse. From this window I used to watch her descend the steps in her riding clothes, snapping the crop against her gathered skirts, stepping into the groom's hand to swing herself onto her hunter. And Papa doesn't shoot now. I have not heard the woods explode in gunfire or seen the birds rise in a panic for ages.

The driver comes round to lift the strangers' luggage down. A great mound of it rises on the gravel. I watch, and so does the cat, its ears like two tiny pyramids, motionless in an ancient Egyptian night. Two people, a man and a woman, climb out of the car. They are dressed any old way, with things on straps slung round their necks. My hand reaches for the silk cord as I watch them stalk up the steps as if they had every right.

Then, worse, someone steps out of the front door to greet them. Some perfect stranger welcomes them into our house.

Still, I am at my post like a sentry standing guard, though we have already been invaded. I don't know how long I cradle the uncomplaining cat who thrusts out a paw and kneads my knee with its bunched claws. It might be moments or hours we sit there. Time means nothing to me when Sebastian is not here.

Then the door of my nursery bursts open with a sound that stings me like a slap. I make quite certain to keep my door shut, now I am older. But it is banged back now, and the driver staggers in under the load of luggage from the car. I shrink behind the curtain, and the cat stands, arching its back, thinking of flight.

Like a dream one can't stop having, the strangers enter my room, the two from the car and the other who let them into our house. Here behind the curtain I can't see them and don't want to, though the room is flooded with sudden light.

"Why, what in the world!" someone says. "Some kind of kid's room?" She is foreign but not blind. She can see the dollhouse Papa made for me, and the rocking horse painted in the colors of Mama's hunter.

"That's right," says another voice, just as common but local. "This was Miss Charlotte's room."

Was and is.

"It's precious!" the foreign voice proclaims. "Isn't it precious? This stuff should all be in a museum, most of it. Shouldn't it?"

But her husband says nothing. He is still gasping from the climb. Six flights to reach my room up here beneath the roof, six flights with a turning at the top.

"And of course it was Mr. Sebastian's, too, when they were both in the nursery. They had a nanny, nursery maids, governesses. Oh, you can't imagine the way people lived then."

"No," the foreign woman murmurs. She is scanning the clutter of my room now. My dolls, propped in corners, gaze unblinking at these intruders. The bear I loved to baldness fixes the invaders with his single eye. "But I don't know if—"

"Well, you see as a rule we don't let this room. But just at the moment, we're expecting quite a large party. Perhaps in a day or so we can find you something on a lower floor."

I am always shy at the first sight of strangers. I edge back, and the curtain moves and they may have seen, so I brush the cat off my lap. It leaps down, spilling itself out below the hem of the curtain, and streaks in the direction of the door.

The foreign woman shrieks.

"Oh, I can't think how that cat got in," she is told. "I opened the window to air the room at midday. Perhaps it climbed the ivy on the walls. Cats do, pesky creatures."

She can't wait to leave the strangers in possession of my room, hoping they will settle. She shows them the device beside the bed

85

that will make their tea, and she opens the cupboard where more blankets are. Then she is gone.

I listen, still as the statues, whilst the strangers make themselves at home, complaining of the cold, remarking on every lump in the bed. "It's not what I had in mind," the foreign woman says, but I hear them opening their valises, and I listen whilst they wander up and down the hall outside in search of the bathroom. The car has gone, and night has fallen. They won't stir themselves, short of morning. They take a great liberty, it seems to me, but I suppose I must put up with them.

But no. They have confused me, and I had almost forgotten that this is the longest night, the night when Sebastian is expected and never comes.

At last the bed wheezes beneath the intruders. Then he must rise again and cross the room on freezing feet to turn off the light.

"I don't think I can figure out how that tea thing works," the woman says in the dark. But then they doze. I can hear them, but it is fitful sleep in a strange bed in a place that does not want them.

The moon appears from behind a scudding cloud, and that suits me well enough. White light plays through the branches of the trees, and moonbeams shatter in the frost on the windowpane. Bright as day, as the saying goes. [Now I must remember the meaning of this night, and who I am, and what I must do.]

For this is the night we learned that we would not see Sebastian again. Oh, I don't mean he didn't come home. Nothing could have kept him away. They brought him home, home from the war, and he is sleeping now, in the churchyard. Cold there, of course, but he feels it no more than I do. Oh yes, Sebastian came home, but not to me who lived for his look, who died to be near him.

They did not take note of how I grieved. Mama rode out, over the hedgerows and through the woods, letting the branches whip her face. She rode like a madwoman who hopes never to heal. Papa shut himself up in his study to pore over the maps of the place where Sebastian fell, as if the maps might be redrawn.

And I was all alone up here, wedged in the window seat, watching for a car in the drive. Until on the longest night of the year I saw the answer plain before my face. The cord that held the curtains.

I looped it over the stout pole from which the curtains hung and wound it round my neck, fixing it tight. Then all I needed to do was spill myself, like the cat, off the high window seat. There was nothing to it. It was only the work of a moment, then forgotten a moment later. Naturally, I could not know that it condemned me to this place forever. That I would remember once again each year on the longest night what I had done, and what I must repeat.

The cord is looped over the pole again. And now I recall how often I have done it before. Oh, eighty times, I should think. With only a little surprise I feel the silken cord that never frays tighten round my neck. I imagine me silhouetted against the glaring moon, and once I have slipped off the window seat, I will swing, head drooped against the frosty night.

How dreadful to awaken in that night and see me there.

BY M. E. KERR

I Will Not Think of Maine

You'd think that he'd be pale, that he'd come from the shadows, that I'd never see him very clearly, but Maine stepped into the kitchen on a sunny Saturday morning looking the same way he always did.

So I said, "I must be dreaming."

I'd dreamed he'd come back maybe a dozen times since his death, but it had been months since I'd had that dream.

In it, he always looked sad. He always said, "I'm so sorry, Zoe. I didn't mean to go that way."

"You couldn't help it," I'd say. "You were so wild, Maine. You weren't like other kids."

Then I'd wake up. I'd feel full of him again. I'd remember how he stood across my room in the dream, with his long hair and his beautiful face, the one skull earring he always wore, the tattoo of the white pinecone and tassel on his arm, the blue-and-white sweatband on his forehead, like the blue and white of his eyes. I'd remember the low purr of his chuckle when something pleased him.

"I dreamed of Maine again," I'd tell my brother.

"Forget Maine, will you, please? He nearly killed Daddy."

Then there he was in our kitchen one summer morning, big as life. Nothing about him said death.

"Are you a ghost, Maine?"

He laughed hard, but it was not a happy sound, not like another boy's laughter. He slapped his knee where his jeans were torn, his hands filled with rings, those silver bracelets he liked jangling down one arm.

He said, "We don't use the word *ghost*. We don't haunt houses or that sort of thing. We call ourselves revenants."

"I never heard that word."

"A revenant is someone who comes back."

Then he did what he always used to do, and it would make my mother furious. He opened the refrigerator door, reached in for the carton of orange juice, put it up to his lips, tossed his head back, and took a long gulp.

"I can't believe it's really you," I finally said.

"Your loving adopted brother is back. Am I your dream come true, Zoe?"

"I guess." I was a little embarrassed to admit it. I *had* thought of him that way. But even though Maine and I weren't related, my family had adopted him and called him "son." After that, I had two brothers.

My family would never have let me date Maine Formann under any circumstances, not just because he was family, but also because he was different from other boys. He looked like some dark, edgy character out of an old English novel filled with moors and dungeons.

89

Back then girls hung out in groups at night, often colliding with boys who did the same.

I could never think of anything to say to one.

They weren't big conversationalists, either.

My mother used to say, "Don't you know why Nelson Rider calls you up all the time, Zoe? He's trying to find the words to ask you out."

"All he talks about is acting in the school plays."

"Invite him over. You'll see."

"What would he do?"

"What do you do when you spend time with Maine?"

"That's different," I said. "I always know what to say to Maine."

The truth was, we hadn't talked that much. But I felt close to him. I felt in some secret way he had the same feeling about me, even though he never said so. I looked out at life through my big thick glasses and waited for things to change.

I was always a major daydreamer, even losing track of what went on in movies I'd watch, because I was thinking of what I'd say one day when Maine came into the theater and just sat down in the empty seat next to me.

Maybe I'd say, "What are you doing here?"

Maybe he'd say, "Well, I knew you were in here so I bought a ticket."

And I'd say . . . never mind what I'd say, or what he'd say. if I had all the hours back I'd spent daydreaming about that sort of thing, I'd be the same age I was then. Thirteen. That was my style, age thirteen. I was waiting for Maine to speak up and tell me what was in his heart.

Mostly, Maine hung out with my real brother, Carl.

They were both fifteen, and neither one was that interested in girls yet.

They liked skateboarding together. They'd go over to Heartsunk

Hill and show off. Carl said Maine was a daredevil, so much so that sometimes Carl thought he was a little crazy. He said it with a tone of admiration, mostly, but occasionally he sounded exasperated, as though Maine went too far . . . like the time Maine brought some beer home he'd gotten an older boy to buy for him. My folks were down at the movies.

He'd shrugged and said, "Your mom doesn't like me drinking your orange juice, so I brought my own refreshments."

Carl told him, "You can drink our orange juice, just don't drink from the container. Put it in a glass."

"I've got my own drink now."

"Don't drink it here or I'll be grounded," Carl said.

Maine had a six-pack with him.

He drank it out in the backyard hammock, singing songs by himself. He got louder and sillier, and the cats ran inside and hid under the bed, and the dog wouldn't stop barking at him.

Then he got really sick. I never saw anyone so sick and sorry, and when my folks got back my father had to put him to bed.

Neither of my folks stayed mad at him. Next day, Mom just said, "That boy is so lost, Zoe. I don't know if we're enough to make up for all that's happened to him. But you're a good sister to him, honey."

"I don't think of him as my brother," I said.

She changed the subject. "Carl says Nelson Rider's in the school play."

"When isn't he? He calls me up and says things like, 'Boy, is my part hard! I've got more lines than anyone.' What am I supposed to say to that?"

"Say, 'Congratulations!' Or say, 'Tell me about the play.'"

"We're all going to see the play so I'll know what it's about soon."

"What would you say if Maine said, 'Boy, is my part hard!'?"

"Maine wouldn't be in a school play," I said. "That's not his style."

"Oh, I saw his style last night. Your father and I came along right in time for the upchucking."

"That's not fair," I said. "And Nelson Rider's ears stick out."

Maine seemed so innocent when he'd sit with me and tell me things he'd like to do someday. He'd say he was going back to Maine where he'd been born, and he was going to live in the woods near a cliff overlooking the ocean.

None of the other boys at school liked Maine. He'd come to us in his freshman year when his parents moved to our town. He'd never connected with a crowd. He shaved his whole head once and painted a happy face on top, with tears dropping from its eyes. He made no effort to get better than passing grades, even though he knew the answers to most every question any teachers asked in classes. He'd tell us school bored him. He complained he missed the weather in Bangor, where he used to live. He missed the bitter cold. Even in freezing weather he wouldn't wear gloves or a scarf or earmuffs like the rest of us.

In falling snow I'd see him with his jacket open, shirt unbuttoned, boots laced only halfway—he had a flair. I envied him that. My mother told me flair and fashion didn't just *happen*—you had to create them for yourself. You had to work at it.

I always doubted there was much I could do with myself. I threw on my clothes and tried not to look in a mirror, because I'd see that I was hopeless.

One day when the family was new in town, Maine's mother showed up at our house looking for him. She was beautiful, and she was driving this white Porsche convertible, and she said, "Tell him his father and I are going to California tonight and we'd like to see him before we go."

Maine could hear her. He was hiding in the hall closet.

When she left, I said, "Wow! Is that your mom? Was that her car?"

Maine said, "You're very impressionable, Zoe."

Carl said, "What do they do in California?"

"They sun themselves," Maine said.

"What does your father do for a living?"

"He makes movies," Maine said.

"Wow!" I said.

"Really?" Carl asked.

"Horror movies," he said. "B movies. . . . You'd think he didn't have a brain in his head."

"But she looks so glitzy, Maine, and she's nice!"

"I'm not close to them. They're always gone."

"Do you ever go with them?" I asked.

"I prefer not to be seen with them," said Maine.

He'd break me up saying things like that. He was cool. I always wanted to be like that: cool.

That morning he showed up in our kitchen, Maine said, "I came back for a reason, Zoe."

"To say you're sorry for almost running over my father?" He was in the hospital for months, and he still limps.

"I shouted at him to get out of the way, Zoe! I tried to brake but it was too late."

"But you were going down *our* driveway in *our* car!"

"I know where I was, Zoe. One thing you always know is where you were when you were born, and where you were when you died." He leaned over and looked out the window. "I died right down the street by that oak tree." Then he socked his palm with his fist. "Pow!" he said. "What a crash! I never drove a car before!"

"I kept dreaming you came back, Maine, and now here you are!"

"Not for long," he said. "I came back on a Saturday morning when I knew your folks would be out and your brother over on Heartsunk skating, and you'd probably be here alone."

I shivered.

"Don't tremble. I'm not going to hurt you. I just want you to stop dreaming about me. Could you please put me out of your head altogether?"

"How did you know I—"

He cut me off. "We always know, because we can't rest if people dream of us. It's been a year now, Zoe. When my family died, I stopped dreaming of them after about a week."

I didn't say the obvious: that he hadn't liked his family, but that I had been crazy about him.

He said, "I had no friends but you and Carl. He's *never* dreamed of me. But you do."

"Yes, I do. Not so much lately but I definitely do."

"Don't!" Maine said. "I don't want to spend the rest of my time in eternity waiting for you to stop dreaming of me. I want to escape life forever . . . to sleep finally!"

"It's just that I always felt so close to you, Maine."

"Don't be like my mother. She had this crush on a rock star she'd never even talked to. After he died in a plane crash, she still kept obsessing about him, even after she got married."

I said, "Am I obsessing? I don't think of it *that* way."

He went right on. "Mother dreamed of him all the time. . . . Then when I was born, I was filled with his spirit. I was born a revenant. That's what made me so different."

"But you said you're a revenant *now?*"

"I was then and I am still. Only now I know what I am. After my encounter with that oak tree down the street I got back my eternal memory. Then I knew why I had never warmed to anyone. It's a revenant trait, you see: we don't warm to live people. Our hearts are so ancient and weary. We feel distanced."

"But you felt close to Carl and me."

"He was the only guy at school who could stand me. So I hung around here. But I didn't feel close to anyone. Not even your parents, and particularly not my parents."

I could feel my heart banging under my blouse, but my voice didn't give anything away. I said, "Did your mother know what you were?"

"Yes. She was warned just as I'm warning you. The rock star told her to let go, that if she didn't he'd return in one form or another, as a revenant."

"Your poor mother!"

Maine threw his head back and roared. "That's a good one! How about poor me? . . . Mommy thought it was fascinating. She even told my father. Anyone else would have thought she didn't have all her marbles, but *he* was fascinated, too. I was their little experiment. They became obsessed with the occult. That happens to people. They get a taste of the eternal and they do strange things: go to seances, hang out with others like them, buy Ouija boards, write creepy screenplays. . . . And they found out everything they could about revenants. They found out that we thrive in cold climates, that it's best to name us after a cold place. Best to stamp cold symbols somewhere on us: a pinecone, a snowbird, something like that. It's supposed to keep us calm."

I stared at his tattoo and felt a chill.

Maine said, "They followed all the rules in the beginning, but I wasn't much like her old rock-star crush. Every revenant needs a spirit to ride back on, but the resemblance stops there. We go our own way, whether we're flesh or vapor." He shook his head, flashed me one of his lopsided smiles. "They just didn't like me. No one really does."

"I did," I said. "I still do."

"It's fading, though. You said so yourself. . . . And that's exactly why I'm here."

Then his blue eyes looked directly into mine. "Say this sentence with me Zoe, okay?"

"Okay."

"I will not dream of Maine."

"I will not dream of Maine," I said.

"Say it over and over to yourself," he said. "Say good-bye forever."

"Good-bye forever."

I looked away, because I didn't want him to see my tears.

When I looked again, Maine Formann was gone.

The only thing I could find on revenants in our library was one paragraph in an occult book. It said the revenant spirit returns sometimes seen, sometimes unseen. Of all ghosts, revenants were the slickest and trickiest.

And I believed it. For what I could not accept was Maine's claim that he did not feel *anything* for me. I told myself it was his way of keeping me from dreaming of him. The only way he could be free was to burst my bubble.

I wanted to be free of him, as well. It was time for me to grow up and get a life. I replaced my thick glasses with contact lenses, began studying *Vogue* when I was at the hairdressers, even suffered through a performance of *The Sound of Music,* with Nelson Rider singing off-key.

Still . . . although there were fairly long breaks between when I allowed myself to think of Maine for more than a pinch of time, often there was a shadow and a glimpse of a bare arm with a white tassel marked upon it, passing through my dreams.

One summer when Carl was home from college, he brought a movie from the video store one night.

"Guess who made it?" he said after dinner, "Maine Formann's father."

"That poor, crazy, kid!" our father said. "May he rest in peace."

"Amen!" I said.

I didn't want to see *Born on Cold Nights*.

I went into the kitchen and stacked the dishes in the dishwasher.

Carl would shout at me from time to time, "Zoe! Come in and watch this! This is weird, Zoe!"

"I'm going out."

"Again?" my father called in to me.

"Again," I said. "And I'm late. People are waiting for me."

"Zoe!" Carl wouldn't give up. "Hey, Zoe! Don't think of a yellow elephant!"

"What is that supposed to mean?" I peered around the corner at my brother.

"This guy playing the revenant says if you tell someone not to do something, they can't help doing it."

Just for a moment, I listened.

"We are revenants with spirits which long to return as revenants. You humans with one life cannot know the joy of life again and again and yet again. Our desire is to return, and your dreaming makes it possible. But what if you stop dreaming of us? How can we prevent that?"

My father shook his head. "Well, we did our best for the boy. But I have to admit that I don't miss him. Do you, Zoe?"

I just shrugged as though it wasn't a question that needed an answer.

Then I left the house, thinking of a yellow elephant, and hearing the low purr of a chuckle somewhere in the vapors of that summer evening.

BY LISA ROWE FRAUSTINO

FRESh PAINt

I admit I didn't do right by Mamie Ellis. Not that I had any choice—I know I did the best I could—but still I feel guilty, letting her down just like everyone else she'd ever loved, after she asked to kiss me good-bye, those dry wallpaper lips on my cheek.

The first of many things that stuck in my mind the day I met her was the FRESh PAINt sign on the foyer wall. The light switch had grimy fingerprints trailing for inches all around it, that's how not-fresh the paint was. Besides that, the "t" was practically falling off the scrap paper the sign was scrawled on, so at first glance I actually thought it said "FRESh PAIN." It was the funniest thing I'd ever seen, a sign saying "FRESh PAIN" in the stale foyer of the Bambrick Mental Health Institute. Then I noticed that a little lower case "t" was there after all, faint and tipped over on its side, and that was even funnier, in a sick way, as if the painter had done it as a joke.

After she'd finished her hide-your-valuables-and-lock-your-car ori-

98

entation talk, the lady who finally answered the door led me through a whole bunch of empty tiled hallways and some locked doors that had to be buzzed open from the other side and made me feel all squeezed-in and panicky. The whole time, I was wishing one long wish that I had never set foot in the place. It felt so spooky, moving like a dream through these empty halls that smelled like a cross between ammonia and cigarette smoke, our foot sounds too loud and dragged out, the door lady's panty hose going *sveep, sveep*. I kept thinking how fat her thighs must be.

We passed nurse's stations and rows of open doors with beds and dressers inside, just plain twin beds and wooden dressers and nothing else—like you'd expect to see in a dorm room where no-body'd moved in yet, except you knew people were living here because they'd be sitting in a chair smoking and staring out the window, or smoking and staring at you walking by, depending on which way they had their chair turned. It freaked me out, realizing that it wasn't just in stories or movies, but people really honest-to-goodness lived like that.

Once the orientation lady looked over her shoulder to stare at me strangely, and I realized I was humming into the silence, a nervous habit I've always had. I bit my lips.

Finally we entered a wing that didn't smell like cigarette smoke. It smelled like my great-grandaunts had just been there. They have this dry, maple-leafy, tragic smell you breathe in when you hug them and your nose goes into their neck or their hair. It made me feel more at home.

The door lady led me to the nurse's desk and said, "May I intro-duce you to Susie MacReavy? She's the talented high school student I told you about who has a school assignment to read to the patients. Susie, this is Nurse Eckman."

Shaking her hand, I remembered how Mama's hand had trembled

as she signed the permission slip, and how I'd lightened the moment by saying, "Mama, if I catch what's going around in there and have to stay awhile, bring me *Cosmo* and plenty of Snickers." Mama had shuddered. Bam Hi—the local nickname for the place—had always given her the creeps, as it did most people around town.

"Good luck," smiled the door lady, and *sveep, sveep,* she was gone. Nurse Eckman grunted, and I followed her down the hall to an activity area where maybe a dozen ancient people were gathered around a television. Some were kind of dressed up; others weren't; a few women had on housecoats like Grammy wears. The only one who looked like she really belonged at Bam Hi had on a miniskirt, old-fashioned nylon stockings falling down around her shins, high-heeled red sandals with toes dancing incessantly, and flaming orange lipstick all over her mouth. That lipstick was so orange, it fought with the red sandals something awful.

The one thing that did seem unusually odd was, none of the patients were talking to each other, not even during commercials. A man in a polka-dotted suit was talking, but he was talking back to the television. Another guy in a ratty blue robe, his mouth was moving like he was talking, only there wasn't any sound coming out. A couple of ladies kept getting up and down, one to look out the window and another just shuffling back and forth with her walker contraption. The walker itself was pretty quiet, but her slippers dragged on the floor making a *scritchety-scratch* sound, and the old guy who was talking without saying anything suddenly yelled like thunder for her to pick up her jeedee feet so he could hear the jeedee television for once, dammitol. At first I didn't know what jeedee meant, but it didn't take long to figure out.

"They're all so . . . old," I said.

Nurse Eckman looked at me as if she was surprised that anyone could be so stupid and said, "Yeah. It's the geriatric wing."

During the next commercial, Nurse Eckman blocked out the television with her hips. The complaints would look even worse written down than they were in real life, so I won't repeat them.

The nurse crossed her arms. "I can stand here all day if you want to keep flapping your traps, or you can shut 'em and listen to what I have to say."

The shouts fluttered into grumbles and finally silence. The jeedee slippers sounded loud again.

"Who here would like to have a story read to them?"

There were a few groans and mutterings among the silent stares, but the woman in the short skirt and falling-down stockings and orange lipstick all over her mouth timidly raised her hand and smiled, sort of but not quite exactly in the direction of Nurse Eckman, toes still dancing like crazy. And I realized it then: she was blind.

"Come on, then, Opal. We'll have story time in your room."

The woman got up and walked straight to Nurse Eckman's voice. You'd never know she was blind if you were just watching her feet; they knew right where they were going. But her eyes, as she came closer, gave it away because they didn't focus on anything, just looked off into a blank wall. They were a faded blue, limp and lifeless, like jeans that have been washed to shreds.

Opal's roommate was sitting in her wheelchair staring at the floor when Nurse Eckman and Opal and I walked into the room. Tiny and wrinkled and brown, her flesh shriveled around sharp bones—I thought of the doll faces we made out of apples in Girl Scouts. Her hair looked glued on and wild, too, but it was a pretty color, pure white without any streaks of yellow or gray. At first I wondered in what decade it had last been combed, but then she put her right hand on her forehead and started shaking her head, her fingers digging in and churning her hair like a rototiller in the garden, and I realized that she and a comb weren't compatible. She still had her head bent

101

toward the floor as she did this, but you could tell she was also looking up at us out of the tops of her eyes.

"Mamie, Mamie Ellis, don't be scared. It's all right, dear!" For once,
Nurse Eckman's voice held a trace of genuine sweetness. If that cod-
fish of a nurse would use such a warm human voice with her, Mamie
Ellis must be someone special.

Suddenly Mamie jolted straight up in her wheelchair, looked Nurse
Eckman in the eye, and said, "I fell and broke my hip. I'll die when I'm
ninety. I'm Mamie. Mamie Ellis. Who's that girl." Such blue eyes she
had, a bright sky blue so intense that it knocked me back a step, or
maybe her voice was the punch—a thick Maine accent like Daddy's
grandfather the lumberjack had, deep and gravelly, certain of itself, almost self-righteous, even, with no question marks in it.

"Yes, Mamie, Mamie Ellis. You broke your hip. But I have a feeling you'll live into the hundreds. Methuselah Ellis, that's you." The
nurse smiled sweetly into those hard, soul-searching eyes. "This is
Susie MacReavy. She's here to read Opal a story. Would you like to
listen, too?"

"I'm in a wheelchair. I fell and broke my hip. That woman's not
happy," Mamie said, squinting and pointing her finger at Opal. "I'll die
when I'm ninety." She already looked a hundred.

"How old are you now?"

Mamie stared at me with those probing eyes as if she were reading something written on the inside of my skull, but she didn't say a
thing, just kept rototilling her hair. It made me nervous, eye contact
with her, like maybe she was seeing something hairy inside me that I
didn't know was there and didn't want to find. I turned to Nurse Eckman and said lightly, "Never ask a lady her age, huh?"

The nurse laughed. "Maybe she'll answer your questions when she
knows you better. Mamie's built a wall around her heart and soul. The

Great Wall of Mamie, I call it. But if you're as stubborn as she is and give it time, she'll pop a rock out to let you peep inside now and then."

"That nurse is talking about me," Mamie said, redirecting her squint and pointing toward Nurse Eckman.

"Well, I have to get back to work. You girls let me know if you need anything."

I gulped and nodded at the nurse's back. It was an intensely lonely moment, like all of eighth grade condensed into one claustrophobic second.

"That woman's crazy. I'm in a wheelchair. I fell and broke my hip. I'll die when I'm ninety," Mamie said. She was looking out the door. The woman with the jeedee slippers was scraping by.

I must have been giggling to myself, because Opal said, "It a funny story you gonna read us, hey?"

Well, that jerked me back to the reality of a report due Monday. I shook my head. "No, Opal. 'The Yellow Wall-Paper' is pretty serious." I cringed, recalling the day I had arrived late to English class after a dentist appointment only to find that the sign-up list for outside performances of our long-rehearsed oral interpretation projects had been passed around and there was only one place left for me—Bam Hi. To read my particular story there seemed like rubbing salt in a wound. But Mrs. Sandrelli enthusiastically predicted that, on the contrary, I would find a very understanding audience.

What an audience. Two octogenarians, one blind, one staring at the floor. With a deep breath, I opened my backpack and took out the script very carefully, because the cover I'd made for it was delicate. For weeks I had searched through all the wallpaper books in town until I found the ugliest yellow design in the world, and all over it I drew bug-eyed women standing on their heads behind the bars, exactly like the poor woman in the story describes it, and finally I took a razor blade and etched little curly tears in the paper so it would look as though it was peeling off a wall.

The story's about a woman writer whose doctor husband keeps her locked in an awful room out in the country away from everyone and won't let her write. He says it's because he loves her so much and wants her to relax to recover from her nervous stress, but Mama says he's a control freak. She says nowadays the woman would go to a shrink for postpartum depression and find out the real reason she's going bonkers is her dysfunctional marital relationship within a dysfunctional society. Maybe. Mama should know.

As I performed the story, Opal cocked her head and listened intently, her mouth and nostrils and cheeks showing every emotion. Mamie looked at the floor and rototilled her hair. The more bored she looked, the harder I tried to become the woman narrating. When I'm really in flow, see, really in sync with my acting, nobody can be bored. They might not like it, but they had to be moved by "The Yellow Wall-Paper," especially at the part where I hum. Grammy couldn't even stand to watch that part, it was so scary. She always had to leave the room.

When I was crawling around on the floor like the narrator is in the end of the story, the hair was standing up on my neck. It was the best performance I'd ever done, and Opal sure appreciated it. She sighed hard and then slowly started to clap. That gave me a rush, but she was an easy audience. It was Mamie's applause I really wanted. Still on my hands and knees, I was at the perfect angle to look straight up into her intense sky-blue eyes and grin at her.

"That woman's crazy," she said. "I'll die when I'm ninety."

That, I realized, was the closest I was likely to get to breaking through the Great Wall of Mamie in one hour. Satisfied, I went home and enriched Mama with the whole story of my day in the geriatric ward of the local loony bin. "Thank God that's over," she said, her voice trembling even more than her hand had been when she signed the permission slip. I hugged her, wrote up my report for Mrs. Sandrelli, and went on with life.

Or tried to.

There was something about Mamie Ellis that got under my hair. I'd be working at a calculus problem and see her blue eyes probing. I'd be cracking an egg and hear her voice saying, "I'll die when I'm ninety." I'd be trimming the hedges and see her bent over in that wheelchair, her fingers raking through her hair. Once in the middle of the night I woke from a dreamless sleep thinking, *Oh my God, Mamie was belted into that wheelchair!* I hadn't made conscious note of it the day I read at Bam Hi, but something inside me must have noticed that the belt she wore around her waist also went around the chair—and it was buckled in back. I lay awake feeling horrified until dawn.

Each time I thought of Mamie Ellis, I wondered more and more about her. She must have been striking when she was young, with those sharp bones and bright eyes. And feisty. What was her life like before she went crazy? How did she end up where she was, why, when, and who put her there? How old *was* she now, anyway? The questions, the questions. Just questions, no answers. It was really getting to me.

It was especially frustrating whenever I had to drive by the Bam Hi entrance on the way to the mall, which was pretty often, since Grammy was always sending me off to Sears for one thing or another. As long as I can remember, Grammy has invited me to "keep her company" on Saturdays, when really she wanted me to take down the curtains to wash, or scrub out the kitchen cupboards, or stack a cord of wood in the basement, or coupon shop until I dropped—the tough jobs she couldn't do with arthritis that looked like speed bumps in her knuckles and knees. I hate all that kind of work, but I love Grammy, so I always went even though I dreaded it.

Mama told me I could say no if I wanted, but how could I? There's this unwritten law in the family: Thou shalt not disappoint Grammy. If you do, you'll never hear the end of it from my great-grandaunts, who raised her after she lost her mother.

The mere mention of her lost mother brought tears to Grammy's eyes, and any words that brought tears to her eyes wouldn't pass through my great-grandaunts' tight lips. Those two skinny-lipped women, when they tighten up, they look like they have no lips at all. Grammy cries at weddings, movies, and the drop of a hat—she cries every time I sing at church, "like an angel, an angel!"—but I've never seen those two cry at anything, not even Grampy's funeral.

One time at a family gathering, I asked who I looked like, and the two of them gasped as if I'd said a four-letter taboo. Grammy was staring at me with a pathetic look on her face, tears brimming.

"What'd I say? I didn't mean . . . I . . . sheesh!"

Great-Aunt Laura patted my hand and said, "You're the spitting image of our poor dead sister, dear, but we don't speak of her. It's too painful for your grandmother." Pain for her would be pain for all of us, so I didn't mention it again.

One Saturday a few weeks after I'd read at Bam Hi, Grammy sent me to the mall for some lightbulbs on sale and, hey, I know this sounds crazy, but as I waited for green at the intersection I could swear the air was thick with that grandaunty smell of the geriatric ward. Before I knew it, I was locking all the cassettes in the glove compartment and humming at the FRESh PAINt sign in the foyer, trying not to feel guilty for doing something that would make Mama tremble if she knew.

Mamie was alone in her room, sitting in her wheelchair, belt buckled in the back. My fingers itched to undo it and set her free, but I stood still.

"I fell and broke my hip. I'm in a wheelchair. I'll die when I'm ninety," she said, rototilling her hair, head down, eyes up. The déjà vu was so strong, it felt as if I'd never even left.

"How old *are* you, Mamie?

She looked up and stared me down again. "I'm Mamie. Mamie Ellis. I'll die when I'm ninety. Who are you."

My heart deflated at the edges. Mamie didn't remember me or my award-winning performance. But hey, she was old, probably losing her memory; she just needed a reminder. "I'm Susie MacReavy, remember? I read you and Opal 'The Yellow Wall-Paper' a few Saturdays ago?"

Mamie peered at the wall of white concrete blocks and shook her head hard, rototilling madly. "Where am I. I'll die when I'm ninety. I'm going to hell."

I gasped. "Why would you say such a thing, Mamie?"

She didn't reply, just stared at me in that intense way of hers, making me squirm, until Nurse Eckman poked her head in the door and said, "Mamie has to go to her physical therapy session now. If you'd like, Susie, you can come along and learn the routine so you can take the old girl for walks. She doesn't get out of her room enough."

As we were wheeling along, I raised my eyebrows and tipped my head toward the horrifying belt buckle. The nurse patted Mamie's shoulder affectionately. "Safety. If she tries to walk on her own—and she will if she can—she'll fall and break her neck."

"But it seems so . . . inhumane. Isn't there some other way?"

After the nurse answered, I was grateful she hadn't laughed at me. "Susie-Q, there are some we have to straitjacket into bed."

We were approaching a concession area where a nurse's aide was kicking a candy machine that kept spitting out her wrinkled old dollar.

"That woman's not happy," Mamie said.

"You wouldn't be happy, either, if you had to live on her salary," Nurse Eckman said, making me smile.

"I'll die when I'm ninety. I like candy, do you." Mamie never once spoke with a questioning lilt in that harsh, monotone voice of hers, and she never smiled the whole time I knew her, but right then her intense blue eyes looked rather impish and hopeful.

Nurse Eckman signaled me to stop the wheelchair. I turned it so Mamie had a panoramic view of the vending machines.

"When I go to college I'm going to major in Snickers," I said. "I'm thinking of minoring in M&Ms or maybe Twix."

Mamie pointed at me and said, "That girl's crazy."

I laughed out loud. "Me? Mamie, that was just a joke. It means I like candy! I'm going to major in music or drama or both."

Nurse Eckman was laughing her peroxide head off, too, until the aide asked her if she had change for a dollar. The nurse clicked her tongue sympathetically and waggled her silent pockets. Then she pulled me aside and whispered, "Mamie doesn't have a penny of her own, and employees aren't permitted to give the patients any special treatment, including treats. If I got caught buying Mamie candy, I could be fired. But if a volunteer were to buy her something, well, that's his or her own business."

During this speech, the nurse was sneaking her hand into her pocket and then out and then into my pocket, and afterward when I put my hand in, there was a dollar bill inside, a crisp one with perfect corners that even the most finicky of candy machines would gobble right up.

I nonchalantly walked over to the machine and said, "So Mamie, Mamie Ellis, is it true what I hear, that you like candy?"

"I fell and broke my hip. I'm in a wheelchair. I'll die when I'm

ninety," she said. Then she pointed to the machine. "They have 3 Musketeers."

"Then 3 Musketeers it is." I whipped out the dollar and grinned.
She probed me with her eyes as usual and didn't say anything else.

Mamie had some trouble unwrapping her 3 Musketeers, and
watching her struggle made my hands ache, because now that they
were out of her hair, I saw how grotesquely twisted her poor fingers
were.

"Here, Mamie, let me help," I said, reaching for the candy. She
snatched it to her chest, scowling fiercely. If she were a dog, I'm sure
she would have bitten my hand off.

I pulled back and apologized even though I didn't know what I'd
done wrong.

Nurse Eckman patted my shoulder and said, "Don't worry about it.
Just learn."

It took Mamie a lot longer to get her 3 Musketeers out of the
wrapper than it did to eat it. As soon as that candy passed her lips,
she didn't stop biting and chewing for one second, not even to
breathe. What awful thing could lie beneath a person gobbling up her
favorite candy and hardly tasting it? I wondered if Mamie'd had to go
hungry a lot when she was a kid. Or maybe things she loved always
got taken away from her.

Mamie would fit nicely into one of the stories Mrs. Sandrelli was
always analyzing with her "tip of the iceberg" theory, which is that
real people and fictional characters are like icebergs. You can only see
the ten percent that shows above water, but it's the hidden part that
sinks ships, so you'd better pay close attention to every detail you
can get.

The next Saturday, I managed to sneak in another iceberg-scouting
visit to Mamie on my way home from Grammy's. "Sneak" is right,

too—I didn't tell a soul where I'd gone, not even my mother. Getting to know Mamie was so exhilarating, I was bursting to tell Mama, but she already had enough to worry about without me aggravating her Bam-Hi-phobia.

The next time I walked in, Mamie said, "You're that girl, ain't you."

"Yes, I'm that girl, Susie MacReavy."

"I fell and broke my hip," she said. "I'll die when I'm ninety. I like candy, do you." On the way to PT, I stopped to buy her a 3 Musketeers bar with my own crisp dollar.

Unfortunately, I wasn't allowed to stay and watch the therapy. To pass the time, I went back to the room and read the newspaper to Opal, who always acted so normal that I asked Nurse Eckman why Opal was even there. "Mental illness tends to burn out with age," she explained. "Opal isn't the only one on the ward who doesn't really need psychiatric care anymore, but there's simply no place else for them to go." I wanted to cry.

And that's the way it went, Saturday after Saturday: "You're that girl, ain't you," the candy, the PT, the newspaper, the challenge of poking at the Great Wall of Mamie. Mostly she said and did the same things over and over, but now and then she'd sneak in something new.

"I'm Mamie. Mamie Ellis. I'll die when I'm ninety. I loved a man named Jim. You have a boyfriend, prob'ly.

"You're that girl, ain't you. I had a daughter. Her name was Lucy. Or maybe it was April. I like candy, do you."

I asked her if Jim or her daughter ever visited her, and she said no. She hadn't seen either of them in years and had no idea where they lived. Maybe Belfast. Maybe the cemetery.

Poor Mamie. She told me she'd had a kitten once. It peed on the floor and her father got so mad, he stood on the kitten and squashed the guts right out of it.

Opal was great; I liked her. But Mamie—Mamie Ellis had some sort of gravitational pull on me, and I thought about her often. "Why does she have to stay belted to that wheelchair week after week after week?" I asked the therapist, who replied, "Stubbornness. Mamie could have been walking weeks ago if she'd use a cane or walker. But every time I drop my guard, she tries to walk alone. We can't risk letting her out of the wheelchair until we're confident that she's safe on her own."

I'd never offer to help Mamie open her candy wrapper, no matter how bad her hands were shaking or how many times she dropped the candy in her lap. You'd think she'd learn to slow down and enjoy it, knowing I'd be back next week to buy more, but she always scarfed up the 3 Musketeers as if it were the first bite she'd had to eat in a week and she was afraid someone would steal it out of her mouth if she didn't swallow it quick.

Whenever I said, "How long have you been here, Mamie?" she'd say, "I'll die when I'm ninety. I'm going to hell."

"How old are you now?" I always asked. It was late December when she actually answered me. "Today's my birthday. I'm eighty-seven." It felt like a Christmas present. I was so excited, I ran straight to Nurse Eckman and jumped for joy. "Mamie told me her age!"

The nurse raised her eyebrows, obviously amused, and congratulated me.

The next time I visited, Mamie told me her age again. She said, "I'm eighty-two."

"Hey," I blurted, "the last time I was here, you said you were eighty-seven!"

"Today's my birthday. I'm eighty-two. I'll die when I'm ninety. I'm going to hell."

I was worried, then, and went to Nurse Eckman again. She laughed at me. "Mamie doesn't know when she was born, Susie-Q. Nobody knows. She's probably in her nineties already, but we always tell her she's eighty-something to keep her spirits up."

It kind of annoyed me that Nurse Eckman didn't tell me all that to begin with, but she's something of an iceberg herself. I think she has a thing about letting people find out for themselves. Maybe her parents bossed her around too much.

During the holiday break, I visited Mamie several times. Friday when I walked into her room, she wasn't there. She was *always* there except for PT and meal times. My heart dropped like a plate. I ran to the desk where Nurse Eckman was calmly doing her paperwork. "How can you sit there like that when something's wrong with Mamie?"

Smiling at her paper, she pointed her nail-chewed stub of a finger toward the activity area. I followed her finger, and there was Mamie, gripping the windowsills for dear life as she inched along, but standing on her own two feet.

"She's walking!" I was stunned.

"She's been at it all morning. If she doesn't sit her butt down pretty soon, I'm going to have to strap her in again."

I ran to her. "Mamie! Mamie Ellis! You're walking!"

"You're that girl, ain't you." She trembled her way to a chair and sat down on it carefully, like it would vanish if she made a wrong move. "I'll die when I'm ninety," she said. "I like candy, do you."

A couple of Saturdays later, Mamie was back in her room, belted into her wheelchair, a cast and sling on her right arm. She was wildly rototilling her hair with her left hand, growling incomprehensibly to herself.

"Mamie! Mamie Ellis! What happened?" I could hardly breathe.

She wouldn't even look at me, wouldn't say one word, just sat there struggling again and again to move that immobilized arm. Having the cast on her wrist must have freaked her out because she wasn't able to rake through her hair with her right hand. She shouldn't be so worried about going to hell, I thought then, because that couldn't be any worse than the life she'd gotten.

At the desk Nurse Eckman handed me the Kleenex and said, "She's had a hard night. Fell on her way to lunch yesterday and broke her wrist. I was hoping your visit would bring her out of it. . . ."

That day on my way out of the building I noticed that the falling-down "t" on the FRESh PAINt sign looked an awful lot like the cross Jesus died on, and the sign didn't seem so hilarious anymore. Made me think of Mamie saying in her monotone, lumberjack-blunt voice, "I'm going to hell. I'll die when I'm ninety."

Mamie was depressed for weeks after that. She retreated so far behind the Great Wall of Mamie, I wondered if she'd ever come back to her peephole. Still, I came by as often as I could, even after school some days, hoping to help bring her back, but she didn't say a word.

As long as Mamie was depressed, I didn't feel much like doing anything except mope about her. Mostly I stayed home and played computer games. I didn't even feel like going out for the spring musical, but I did it anyway so Mama and my teachers wouldn't freak. Mama was having enough of a fit as it was, forcing food on me when I had no appetite, so I gained ten pounds in all the wrong places without even enjoying it. She spent hour after hour whispering about me to Grammy and the great-grandaunts after I went to bed, which I knew because I wasn't sleeping well. Sometimes it felt like I hadn't slept at all, but I knew I must have because in the morning I'd remember strange dreams as vividly as waking life.

One dream kept repeating itself. I was looking through the empty halls of Bam Hi for Mamie and couldn't find her. Every time I'd pass a room, I'd see a flash of movement and run in to see if it was her—but the only person I'd see was myself, in the mirror, naked. Again and again, there I was, naked as a newborn, and it shocked and embarrassed me every time, but I couldn't stop to find any clothes because I had to keep looking for Mamie. Did the dream mean I could find myself at Bam Hi (seeing myself in the mirror), or that I couldn't find myself there (because I couldn't find Mamie Ellis)?

Finally, around six weeks after she broke her wrist, Mamie looked up at me and said, "You're that Varney girl, ain't you." The new word in her greeting shocked the breath out of me.

Varney was my grandmother's maiden name.

"Mamie! Do you know my grandmother, Norma? Norma Varney?"

"I'll die when I'm ninety," Mamie said. "That woman's crazy. I like candy, do you."

So Mamie was back to normal, pretty much, except every time I came to visit, she'd say, "You're that Varney girl, ain't you," and I'd try (but fail) to pry the connection to my grandmother out of her.

I had several theories. Maybe Grammy used to hang out with little Lucy or whatever Mamie's daughter's real name was, but I still couldn't understand why Mamie would confuse me for Grammy. She and I don't look a bit alike, except for the thick ankles that run in the whole family. My great-grandaunts were of the same generation as Mamie, but they weren't Varneys. Their sister had married the last one. Mamie might have known her, or—Wouldn't this be neat: What if Mamie herself was the Varney connection, some long-lost black sheep relative? I actually got excited about that one, until I realized it was too far-fetched even for an insane asylum. No, my great-grandma Varney had to be the missing link.

Mama was willing to talk about her grandmother, but she didn't know much. Or so she said again one Saturday when I asked her for the hundredth time. She was matching socks in the living room.

"Sheesh, Mama. Weren't you ever just burning with curiosity about her? Your own flesh and blood and recessive genes? Didn't you ever grill the greats about her?"

Suddenly she leaped up with my athletic sock and swatted a cobweb out of the ceiling fan. Then she looked at me and said, "My great-aunts have always been very good to my mother and me. Their feelings are more important than any curiosity I have about their sister."

"Oh-kay. What about Grammy, then? Didn't she ever tell you anything about her mother? She must have let *something* slip now and then when you were growing up."

Mama was pacing the room now, swatting away with the sock. "No. Well, yes. Here's something. She sang. Mama said my grandmother sang all the time." Mama's thin, quavery voice sounded nervous. I tried to catch her eye, but the cobwebs had her.

"Sang? That's it?"

"That's what my mother said."

"Like me? Did she sing soprano?" I was getting excited, now.

Mama turned to me, stiff, the sock of doom dangling pathetically off the hip where her fist was perched. "I haven't a clue, Susie. I don't know what she sang. I don't know anything else I can tell you, and Grammy's waiting for you anyhow. The dead flies have piled up in her glass lights."

In the end I discovered the truth the way most family secrets spill out—by accident. It happened at my high school graduation party. The day was rainy, so we had to set all the tables and chairs up in the garage instead of outside as originally planned to avoid a lobster mess in the house. The garage isn't that big, and my extended family is, so it was sensory overload. The place smelled like the geriatric ward of Bam Hi until the lobster started boiling and took over the airwaves. We were in the middle of cracking claws and tails, lobster guts spewing all over, including all over my glasses, when this pigeon-toed pudge of a distant cousin I hardly even know popped out with, "Hey, Susie-Q, how come you didn't wave to us that day in the car?"

"Gee, Wes, I don't know. Might be because I didn't see you. What day do you have in mind?"

"A'course you seen us. Me and Ash was setting in the Blazer right across from you at that forever-red light down near the mall. We was waving and honking at you like crazy. Ash even waited after the light changed so you could make your turn ahead of the traffic jam. What was you doing coming out of Bambrick Mental, anyways?"

All of a sudden it was so quiet, you could have heard a jeedee slipper scuffing across the garage floor. The kids all gaped at each other as if Wes had said I was going to jail for murder, and the older folks all gasped and held their breaths as if they were bearing down against some awful stomach pain. Grammy looked meaningfully at Great-Aunt Laura and Great-Aunt Mary Joyce. Their eyes were positively panicky—a deer-in-headlights moment if I ever saw one.

Grammy pulled the fork across her teeth with an excruciating scrape and said to me, "You were at Bambrick?" She had almost no voice at all.

I think I must have nodded, stunned into silence by their over-reaction.

"I'm sure she was just turning the car around there," Grammy said to her aunts in a high voice. "You know how the traffic can be out that way."

There was a long silence until Great-Aunt Laura cleared her throat and said, "Were you turning the car around, Susie?"

I think I must have shaken my head.

Mama was looking everywhere except in people's eyes, smiling nervously, holding up the canner pot. "Would anyone like another lobster? Fresh batch! Susie and I bought them straight off the lobster boat first thing this morning. We . . ." While she's doing the longest soliloquy since Hamlet, Mama's madly dumping lobster parts on any

116

empty plate she can see. Suddenly she looks up and beams, positively beams at me.

"Of course! I remember now! You went to Bam Hi—I mean Bambrick—to do that school assignment! See—" she nods at Grammy and the great-grandaunts— "Didn't I tell you?" Grammy's shaking her head, but Mama's full speed ahead. "Susie had to go there to perform a story, the one that won the regional speaking competition, remember? Back in the fall? She got an A plus plus on that project. I'm so proud of my baby, all grown up now, near the top of her class and heading off to college in the fall. . . ."

Voices and plates resume their clattering. The weight of the family's curiosity has lifted off my chest and I can breathe again—until that cowlick head Wes says to me in a confused voice, "But Susie, if you was reading that story over to Bambrick Mental in the fall, how come you didn't wave to me and Ash when we seen you there *last Saturday?*"

Mama and Grammy are stretching out over their plates so far, waiting for my answer, that they look like they're floating. I feel like I've just stepped out on stage, only this time I'm playing the part of myself and don't know my lines. I should have rehearsed. I should have known that this day would come, that the truth would leak out eventually and I'd have to find words to explain.

"I . . . oh sheesh. Bam Hi—Bambrick—makes people so nervous. . . . Just look at you all now, the horror the horror. This is exactly what I was afraid of! I didn't tell anybody because I didn't want Mama or Grammy or the aunts to worry about me spending so much time at a mental hospital."

The air seems yellow, thick, wavy with nervousness. Somebody lets out a little involuntary scream. Maybe it's me.

"Wait! I don't know what you're all thinking, but I'm not going to

Bambrick Mental Health Institute for *help* or anything like that. It's not *bad* that I go there. I've been volunteering! That's all! Every Saturday! I stop there on my way to or from Grammy's so I can help out in the . . . in the geriatric ward. They don't have enough help there, see, and those poor people, they—they don't have anyone to love them, and I felt so sorry for them when I met them that day when I read 'The Yellow Wall-Paper' there. They needed someone. If you could see them, you'd know what I mean. If you could see Mamie. . . . Mostly I work with this one old lady named Mamie. Mamie Ellis."

I looked beseechingly into the eyes of my family. Mama puts her arm around me, pulling me close and caressing my forehead, but Grammy and the great-grandaunts looked stunned. They're staring into the yellow air with their mouths open.

I'm starting to think my confession has crashed into the tip of one monster mama iceberg.

My mother gazes around intensely, smiles like the sun coming out and points out the garage door. "Look! The rain's burned off! How about if everyone dishes up some strawberry shortcake and takes it outside?"

To me she whispers, "Let's take ours in."

The crowd doesn't hesitate to take their cue. Even cousin Wes plays his part, racing to the dessert table and making chatter about the weather on his way. Meanwhile, Mama gently pulls Grammy by the elbow and gestures for me to do the same with the aunts. We move in slow motion to the living room and sit awkwardly, toes jiggling like Opal's, all of us looking up and biting down words, none of us wanting to be the first to speak. Finally Mama breaks the iceberg.

"Don't you think it's about time you told her the truth? And me the whole truth? She has—*we have*—a right to know." Mama leans over to look deeply into Grammy's eyes and says, "What did she sing, Mama?"

Great-Aunt Laura gasps. "Do you really want to spoil Susie's special day by bringing out dirty laundry?"

Grammy doesn't even look at Aunt Laura. Waves of every emotion imaginable ripple across Grammy's face. Finally she smiles, just a little, into Mama's eyes. Her head rises and her body straightens. She looks a foot taller. "If it must be done, I can't think of a better time. But dirty laundry!" Grammy directs an unambiguous scowl toward her aunts. "Must we think of it that way?" She nervously runs her hand through her hair, once, not nearly rototilling, but it's still enough for me to think of Mamie.

"Dirty laundry," I mutter, shaking my head. I'm feeling as horrified as I did in that middle of the night when I realized Mamie had been belt-buckled into her wheelchair.

Mama hops up and paces along the pattern in the oriental rug, a habit she developed when she used to wait up all night for Daddy. "Dirty laundry that's not out on the line to air, understand, Susie. It's packed away in an old chest in the attic and left there to rot."

"So is this dirty laundry a shirt? Or a pair of pants? A dress? I know, it's a bra and underwear!"

Nobody laughs at my nervous joke. Mama's left eye is twitching. She rubs her temples before going on in an eerily calm voice. "All these weeks and months you've been volunteering at the mental hospital, helping with an elderly woman—"

"Mamie," says Aunt Mary Joyce, almost mournfully.

"Mamie Ellis," Aunt Laura adds.

"You know her?" My heart is beating so fast and furious, it hurts. Grammy's hands, Mamie's. Could we be related after all?

"She and I were in the same school before she had to quit," Aunt Laura says. "Lord, the bruises that girl used to wear . . . sometimes we wondered how she could move a muscle. Nary a word she'd say about it, but we all knew it had to be her no-good father. God only knows what else he did that nobody could see."

I think of Mamie's kitten.

Aunt Mary Joyce picks up the story. "It's no wonder she took up with that no-good Jim-Something from down Portland way. She was only sixteen when she ran off to have the baby."

It's no wonder Mamie thinks she's going to hell, I'm thinking. Unwed pregnancy was the ultimate taboo in those days.

"That was the last we saw of her until years later when we . . . ah—" Aunt Laura's eyes roll upward as she searches the corners of her mind for the right word. There's something she is still trying hard not to tell me. What is it? Mamie's related? Is she? My heart can't take much more.

"—we *discovered* she'd had a nervous breakdown."

The great-grandaunts stare wordlessly at Mama's feet tracing the rug pattern.

"Discovered," I say.

Grammy takes my hand and squeezes it. She clears her throat and says slowly and clearly to the aunts, "I imagine you must have discovered that this woman was at Bambrick when you were there visiting Mama."

As my mother spins in the middle of the carpet to face Grammy, it feels like I'm swimming in cloudy water, trying to see something without enough light. It takes a couple of seconds to sink in that I'm looking at the bottom of the iceberg. *Grammy's mother—Mama's grandmother—the great-grand-aunts' sister—my great-grandmother— was in Bam Hi with Mamie. That's the Varney connection.*

It made such perfect sense, I wondered if some deep-inside part of me had known the truth all along and drawn me to Mamie as much as Mamie herself had.

Mama breathed hard and took a decade letting the air back out before she explained. "Your great-grandmother did die young of cancer, as you were always told. We just didn't tell you that she was in Bambrick at the time. She was only in her twenties when she was committed. She spent the last thirty years of her life there. We didn't tell you because . . . this is hard to say."

But I already knew. "Because I look so much like her on the outside, you were afraid I might have her crazy genes inside, too? And maybe even more afraid that my knowing about it might make it come true?" The connections were coming fast, now. "You were protecting me from myself, my own fear, the same as I was doing for you when I didn't tell you I was volunteering there."

Grammy was sniffling now. "That's all part of it, dear, but—" Aunt Mary Joyce clicked open her big beige clasp purse and pulled a lace hanky out for her. Grammy dabbed her eyes.

"We watched all three of you," Aunt Laura said, "for signs, growing up. But Susie was the only one who sang."

"She sang everything," Aunt Mary Joyce said. "Sang or hummed, all the time. Hardly ever talked."

"On pitch, too," Mama said proudly, squeezing my shoulders.

"I mean Avis," said Aunt Mary Joyce. "Our sister."

"My mother," said Grammy. "Susie, from the time you were born you looked and acted so much like her, to the point that . . . well, it was downright uncanny. And scary. We just didn't see any sense in having that on your mind to worry about, dear. Being a teenager is hard enough as it is, always wondering how you fit in, lying awake night after night trying to figure out if it's the whole world that's nuts or if it's just you."

"Well, we do know it's not you, honey," Mama added quickly. "You've had your down times, but everyone does. So far you've handled the loo-loo slings and arrows better than most. Even this spring when you had the doldrums, you got through it on your own and came out stronger on the other side."

I blushed. "I was depressed because Mamie was. I couldn't do anything to help her, and it was overwhelmingly frustrating."

"That's the way it always is when we can't protect loved ones from pain," Aunt Laura said in a thin voice.

I thought about her and Aunt Mary Joyce watching me and Mama and Grammy for crazy signs. "Remember the year I was thirteen? Totally loo-loo."

"I remember. That year you were a normal, turbulent teenager. It was your father who was loo-loo," Aunt Laura said. Mama snorted a laugh.

That was all it took for me to start giggling. Giggling that Aunt Laura called Daddy loo-loo. Giggling at the irony of how I ended up at Bam Hi after all—not to be locked up like my great-grandmother or even to find traces of her but to try to poke a rock out of the Great Wall of Mamie. Giggling so I wouldn't cry when this little voice inside me screamed *How could my family keep their history a secret from me? How could they keep me apart from a piece of who I was?*

Like a dream, I imagined Grammy and Mama at my age, impossibly driving together past Bam Hi, wondering if they'd end up living and dying there some day, questioning whether this or that off thing they'd said or done or felt meant they were crazy. What a terrible burden it was, this knowing. . . .

Gradually the giggling turned to tears, good clean tears of release and forgiveness. Mama was sharing Grammy's lace hanky, and I'd soaked the one from Great-Aunt Laura's purse, but the great-grandaunts were still dry-eyed. I figured they'd probably cried this all out years ago.

"So what did she sing, anyway?" I asked.

Grammy sighed, smiled, settled back into the couch. "I vaguely remember hearing her voice soaring above the others in church. Soprano. Like a bird. But mostly I remember she'd just *sing*. Sing the things she wanted to say, with no particular melody. Like, 'now it's time to wash our face, now it's time for flowers to hug the sun.'"

Wow, I thought. Wow. How incredibly creative and . . . interesting. I wish I could have known someone like that. And this was *my* great-grandmother. Mine!

"Was she pretty?" I asked.

Everyone laughed at me. "Go look in the mirror, Beauty," said Great-Aunt Laura.

"Beautiful inside and out," Great Aunt Mary Joyce said. "And we couldn't do a damn thing to—"

Well, that did it. Aunt Mary Joyce looked at Aunt Laura, Aunt Laura looked at Aunt Mary Joyce, their stiff faces went limp, and the two of them fell into each other's arms. They burst into tears that shook their bodies. They cried and cried and cried and didn't even bother with hankies.

Grammy nodded at Mama. The two of them smiled pained little smiles and Mama said, "Better late than never."

After that the summer passed quickly. I got a job at Bam Hi as an aide, cleaning rooms and helping with patients. Sometimes I caught myself humming on the job and wondered about my sanity. I'd never been so self-conscious about my humming habit before, and with a flash of understanding I appreciated what my family had done, trying to protect me from unnecessary self-doubts. Lots of people hum. Don't they?

I had plenty of opportunities to ask Mamie about my Great-Grammy Avis, but she never had anything to say on the subject except, "You're that Varney girl, ain't you." Nurse Eckman sneaked me down to the hospital archives to look for her records, but we didn't find anything.

Grammy did tell me what little she could remember of her early childhood before "the nervous breakdown." That's what she and her aunts insisted on calling it, no matter what logical explanations of mental illness I gave. To her it would never be like ulcers or coronary heart disease or cancer—a common illness. It was a stigma.

She remembered her mother was very lovely and very sad, not much of a talker except for what she sang. Grammy was her only child, but she had several miscarriages. The day of the last one, she started singing and wouldn't stop. She sang for weeks and weeks until finally her husband put her in the car and the aunts moved in and that was that. Grammy never saw her again. Did my great-grandmother keep singing for thirty years once she got to Bam Hi? I wonder.

Grammy has thanked me over and over for helping her bring back the memories she'd pushed down. It's like a piece of her mother is alive again, she says. And locked up inside the great-grandaunts, I know there's an even bigger piece of the woman who sang. I'm not going to give up looking for it. I need it. And they need it, too. All of that guilt and grief they feel would be better out than in.

As for Mamie, I loved her more than ever.

After her wrist healed, she was only allowed out of the wheelchair if she promised to use a walker. Nurse Eckman even got special permission for us to stock up on miniature 3 Musketeers bars so we could give Mamie one as a reward every time we caught her using her walker correctly. Mamie cleaned us out of candy twice the first week, but she must have finally gotten her fill because after that she kept shoving the walker aside and taking off on her own. It wasn't long before she fell and broke her ankle. So she was back in the wheelchair for good by the time I had to break the news that it was time for me to head off to college.

I'll never forget the look on Mamie's face when I told her.

Even though she never smiled, Mamie always had this hopeful look on her face whenever I walked in, a pert look that said, "You're mine and I'm yours and we like candy." The moment I told her I was leaving for college, her whole face fell a good inch, and only then did I realize how much her spirits had risen in the months after her broken wrist. The broken ankle hardly phased her—she still had her rototilling hand.

"That Varney girl's going away," she said. "I'll die when I'm ninety."

"How old are you now, Mamie?" I still always asked.

"Eighty-nine. Kiss me good-bye."

My heart veering, I leaned over and kissed her cheek. It smelled very great-grandaunty.

"Do you want to kiss me, too?" I asked. She nodded, and I leaned down so she could peck my cheek with her dry lips, peeling like yellow wallpaper.

"I'll die when I'm ninety. That woman's unhappy. I'll never see you again," she said, rototilling madly.

I suppressed my urge to laugh at her silly paranoia and said gently, "Mamie! Mamie Ellis, you know better than that. I'll always visit you when I come home!"

She stared me down in her Mamie-esque way and said, "You'll visit me when you come home. I'll die when I'm ninety. I'm going to hell."

College was only a couple of hours' drive away, and I really did have good intentions of coming home weekends to visit Mamie and keep Grammy company, too. But I made some really interesting friends at college, including a guy, okay? And got a good role in a play, with rehearsals every night, including weekends. Plus there was studying to do, much more of it than in high school. Life took up a lot more time than I had expected. But Mamie would understand, I told myself, and we'd both enjoy our stolen moments together all the more, once I got a chance to explain.

By the time I got that chance, it was Thanksgiving break. The FRESh PAINt sign was still in the Bam-Hi foyer, attracting spiders, and as soon as I got inside I asked Nurse Eckman why somebody didn't take that sign down already. She laughed sarcastically and said, "Go ahead and fill out a work order, honey," patting my shoulder as if I were a cute child. But then she got really serious on me, wet-eyed serious, and I knew something was wrong.

"I thought you were going to call me if anything happened to her!" I was feeling all panicky again, like the time I thought Mamie had died but really she'd just gotten out of her wheelchair and was walking around the activity room.

The nurse nodded. Jet black hair, this time, with purple highlights. "And I will. It's just that Mamie didn't take it very well after you left, Susie-Q. She watched the door for weeks, waiting for that Varney girl, and after she realized that you weren't going to show, she stared at the floor and refused to talk to anyone. It was as if she'd broken both arms. She's just now started talking to me again. I know you love her, dear, but. . . ."

"Well, don't you think she'd be glad to see me now? I brought her a whole box of 3 Musketeers bars—Halloween clearance sale."

Nurse Eckman dabbed her eyes with a tissue. "If you really need to see her, I won't stop you. But think hard about it."

It didn't take much thinking. If I visited Mamie now, it would make us both happy for a few minutes, but then what? I'd go back to my friends and my boyfriend and my play and my books while she went back to looking at the door until her face dropped.

I truly hated myself at that moment of decision. This was a terrible thing I'd done to Mamie Ellis—making her love me, and then disappearing. I hadn't meant to mess up her life like that. I loved her, too. But life just got so terribly, I don't know, complicated. Why did it have to be that way?

126

Doing the right thing was hard, the hardest thing I've ever done, but I did it. I put the box of 3 Musketeers on the nurse's desk and walked briskly out of the geriatric ward, through the maze of corridors, and almost out the foyer door forever, except something about the FRESh PAINt sign made me stop. It seemed different somehow, in a subtle, hard-to-place way, like when your boyfriend changes his earring. I studied the sign hard until it came to me: somebody had whited out the "t". So now the sign read FRESh PAIN after all.

Passport

I returned to the Land of Mom with a bag of dirty clothes and a hang-over.

It was a small, ruffled country. Smelled like bleach.

I was the only person allowed in both nations: the Land of Mom and the Kingdom of Dad. They were once a united empire. But a rev-olution broke out, a bloody two-year conflict that divided the empire forever. The peace treaty had been signed six months earlier. I shut-tled back and forth, a six-foot-two Demilitarized Zone with bad skin.

My mission was to maintain diplomatic relations with both parents until graduation. After that? Classified information. Let's just say I had other plans.

The Land of Mom had its own set of customs, a hatchling language, and a unique culture. There was the traditional embrace.

She rushed at me, squealing. I set down my duffel bag and opened my arms. She yanked my face to her shoulder and clenched me in a respectable headlock. Thumped me hard on the back, as if trying to get up a burp. We rocked violently from side to side. More thumping. Then the sudden release.

"I've missed you so much!" she said.

"I was gone two days."

She grabbed my wrist and dragged me to the kitchen.

"I made meat loaf for dinner and beets and baked potatoes. And I got real sour cream for you—I know how much you hate the fat-free."

Mom thought I loved meat loaf. God knows where she got this twisted idea. I hated it. I'd rather push in next to Abby Tabby Kitty and crunch on kibble than slog through ground cow with ketchup.

But food in foreign countries is symbolic. Tied up with history and values. How could I refuse the meat loaf without provoking an international incident?

"Meat loaf—you didn't have to do that! I'm really sorry, but Dad and me already ate. I'm stuffed. I better get started on my homework." (Translation: *Please let me out of here before I heave on the linoleum.*)

"But it's meat loaf, your favorite!" (Translation: *You'd rather eat junk with your scum father than eat food I cooked with my own hands.*)

Guilt. Another ritual in the Land of Mom.

I kissed her hair spray and took a plate out of the cupboard.

"I'll eat dinner at my desk. Thanks for thinking of me." (*I'll flush dinner down the toilet. Please let me go to sleep.*)

Abby Tabby Kitty, the foul beast, lifted an eyebrow. The cat had psychic powers and picked up on all translations. I would have to buy her silence with some meat loaf.

Mom patted my cheek.

"You're a good son, Jared."

———

The Kingdom of Dad was price-tag new. Every time I visited, I'd dig out the toenail clippers to snip off a few more labels from Macy's. Dad took only his CD-player and golf clubs when he left. He was "starting fresh."

I was allowed one weekend in the Kingdom of Dad every two weeks. Arrival called for a ritual welcome dance.

"Hey, Dad." I lightly punched him in the arm.

"Hey there, boy!" He punched me back, harder.

We both crouched in imitation of professional fighters. Dad broke his stance first.

"Come on in. Wait till you see what I got."

Another toy. This time it was a cell phone that he wore in a leather holster on his hip. My dad, gadget dude.

I stowed my duffel bag behind the couch. His condo only had one bedroom, so I slept on the fold-out. I flicked through the cable channels and hunted through the magazine bin for the take-out menus.

Dad opened two beers in the kitchen.

"Talk to Sergeant Payne about boot camp yet?"

Sometimes Dad didn't need translating.

I turned up the television and mumbled something.

He handed me a beer and threw a bag of Doritos on the couch.

"Boot camp," he declared, hand on his cellular.

Vienna, I thought. Diplomats in Austria have confrontations like this in ballrooms full of waltzing women and waiters carrying champagne. Somebody asks a tough question, you reach for the caviar and flirt with the Swedish consul.

No caviar in the Kingdom of Dad. Think, think.

"I'll be honest—I haven't had time, Dad. My senior project, work, helping Mom; I haven't talked to the sergeant yet. But it's at the top of my list." (*I will enter the army when pigs fly. Get a clue and leave me alone.*)

He cracked his knuckles and checked his watch.

"Get it done soon. Don't want you hanging around like a waste-case this summer. The army will make you a man." (*The army will pay for college so I won't have to give up the Porsche.*)

Crisis delayed. I held out the Doritos, a peace offering.

"Want me to pick up a movie? I'll get us pizza while I'm out."

Dad cleared his throat. "Actually, I have a guest coming."

He glanced at his watch again. Rolex. Good down to five hundred feet underwater. No price tag to cut off, but give him half a second, he'll tell you how much it cost.

I looked at my watch. Sears. Ran slow when I stood close to the microwave. Present from Aunt Betsy. Who was this guest, Sergeant Payne?

The doorbell rang. Dad bolted. I changed channels. The Bulls were supposed to be playing. Dad talked to someone at the front door. He called my name. No Bulls anywhere. Maybe hockey.

"Jared Michael." (*Put down the damn remote and pay attention.*)

I looked up.

"This is Heather."

(*There's nothing in the dictionary about this! 911! 911!*)

Heather was a goddess. No, more than a goddess—she was a centerfold. No, she didn't look sleazy. A body with Indy curves and long straight-away legs, thick blond hair that framed the face of an angel. I glanced at the television. She had to be a *Baywatch* fantasy teleported to Dad's living room. Except I was still watching hockey.

In a panic, I stared into the Doritos bag. All my years in cross-cultural studies had not prepared me for this. My father: accountant, bald, dumpy, owned a great car. His date: Lust of my Life.

What was wrong with this picture?

Stealth attack on the Land of Mom. Villagers running through their wheat fields screaming. Cities collapsing, forests ablaze.

131

Mom, meet Heather. Heather, this is Mom.

Dad masterminded the plan, a bombing raid under the cover of "dropping off Jared." Heather wore a T-shirt cut real high and shorts that drooped wonderfully low. A tanned relief map of abdominal muscle connected the two scraps of cloth.

Mom wore one of Dad's abandoned robes and slippers that looked like something Abby Tabby Kitty had coughed up. Heather held out her arm to shake hands, and a million silver bracelets jingled.

Mom slammed the door. Heather squeaked. Dad chuckled. They drove off laughing with the top down.

Like I said, a stealth attack.

Mom sat at the kitchen table, drinking glass after glass of skim milk. A gang of goldfiches swooped toward the birdfeeder and drove off an ugly starling. The cat watched the window, saliva dripping down its chin. Abby Tabby Kitty wanted bird for lunch. Mom understood the feeling.

I talked about the weather; the radio guy promised rain. No response. I lied about getting recommendation letters from my teachers. Nothing. Didn't even get a smile. So I told the truth.

"I think he's being stupid."

She took a long drink of milk and slammed the glass on the table.

"I don't want you to tell me anything." (*Tell me every nasty detail about that slut.*)

"There's nothing to tell." (*If I get in the middle of this, I'm going to get my head blown off.*)

I poured a glass of real milk, took a bag of Oreos out of the cupboard, and sat at the table. Mom piled ten cookies in front of her. She was hungry. A good sign. I watched closely for tears, but saw nothing.

"She'll give him a heart attack, mark my words." She grinned, evil but cute. This was positive, a new development.

We twisted, we dipped, we munched. Oreos are sacramental snack food. The border skirmish had wounded her, but it wasn't a fatal blow. Perimeter secure, no need to call in reinforcements.

Halfway through the bag, she took some thick envelopes off the pile by the phone.

"I wrote for more applications."

They landed in my lap like a Scud missile. State colleges, community colleges. All an easy drive away.

"I don't need to apply anywhere else," I said. "Want another cookie? A Ring-Ding?" (*Please, please, please change the subject.*)

"Of course you need to apply somewhere else." (*With your grades you'll be lucky to get in anywhere.*)

"I still think a year off . . ." (*Paris, Mom. I want to go to Paris. And London. And Prague, Munich, and Copenhagen.*)

"Send them in." (*Subject is closed. I'm the Queen and you will obey.*)

She tilted her head and squinted at the window.

"Do you really like those curtains? I'm getting tired of all that lace."

The Kingdom of Dad had been invaded.

Heather's clothes filled the closet. Her stockings graced the shower. The sink was hidden under makeup and bottles of colored goo. And we had to put the seat down.

The kitchen had no food. Corn chips—gone. Tasty-Kakes—gone. Buffalo wings—way gone. The top shelf of the fridge was for bottled water, the rest given over to carrots and lemons.

I stretched out on the couch (new white couch that doesn't fold out) to watch the Bulls. All I could see were Heather's trim ankles, Heather's sleek calves, Heather pumping her legs up and down on her exercise bike in front of the television.

I was lusting after my Dad's girlfriend. This had to be a sin—it felt too weird.

The Kingdom of Dad was issuing press bulletins to his golfing buddies. He bellowed into the cell phone while Heather aerobicized.

"Never been happier!"

"Nothing like a twenty-one-year-old to make you feel young!"

"What was the number for that hair replacement surgeon?"

My duffel bag waited in a corner of the kitchen. The college applications peeked out of the top. They accused me, spies sent from the Land of Mom to keep me on the straight and narrow path.

I went through the mail. I used the Kingdom as my return address for the stuff I really cared about. Dad didn't open my mail. Dad didn't open his own mail. If a terrorist sent a letter bomb to the Kingdom, it would rust before it blew up.

It hadn't come yet. Another two weeks of waiting stretched out, Antarctic journey on cross-country skis.

Heather toweled fragrant drops of perspiration off her forehead. Would she notice if I kept the towel? She leapt off the bike and trotted for the shower. She stopped to plant a kiss on Dad's bald spot.

"The mall?" she asked.

He nodded.

This was my moment. Heather was chirping in the shower and Dad still feeling tingly from that kiss. Mom wanted me to apply to King Dad for financial aid. The Land of Mom was a developing nation—the Kingdom of Dad was loaded. Guess who had the better divorce lawyer.

But Heather bounced out of the bathroom, clean and damp. The mall awaited.

We shopped. We compared The Limited to Express, Nordstrom to Bloomies. Who knew perfection was so difficult? We shopped some more. Dad waved his Gold Card, I carried the bags.

When Heather was exhausted, we stopped for lunch at the

Anorexic Cafe. Heather ordered a parsley salad and cabbage juice. Dad ended up with a baked tomato. I munched on breadsticks stolen from surrounding tables.

I asked Heather if she had any friends she could fix me up with. I figured it would be less of a sin if I dated a pseudo-Heather.

She was about to recite names, numbers, and vitals, but Dad shook his head.

"He's too young," he growled. (*I can date a girl your age, son, but you can't. It's good to be the King.*)

Fortified by forty-five calories, Heather was ready to shop again. She needed new shoes, then a hat, then a brooch. Never did find out what a brooch was. In the jewelry store, she threw her arms around Dad with a high-pitched hiccup.

She had an Idea. Dad and I should both get an ear pierced.

He almost did it. He had been saying "Sure, honey" all day. But he caught the reflection of his bald spot off a million shiny surfaces. He shook his head to clear it of the pixie dust.

The King took control. No earrings.

Heather pouted. Dad promised her that brooch thing, whatever it was. She sulked. Dad mentioned a motorcycle jacket. Heather's bottom lip jutted out. Tears threatened.

Dad promised a fur coat.

The sun came out from behind the clouds. They paraded out of the jewelry store, the brooch a memory. I trailed behind.

She had him. She had him hooked, reeled in, gutted, and mounted on a board to show her friends. Heather was after the Crown. She wanted to be the new Queen.

She stayed at the condo while Dad took me back to Mom's. We stopped at Taco Bell for real food. Burritos, nachos, soft tacos, hard tacos, spicy meat, liquid cheese. Coke—all the sugar and all the caffeine, thank you.

The King and I grunted with pleasure as we ate. Cro-Magnon communication. Two guys eating greasy food. We didn't talk about anything. It was perfect.

I ruined the moment with the plea for financial aid.

"We discussed this at the alimony hearing. You're going into the army. It made me the man I am today, plus they'll pay for school. Any more hot sauce?"

I tossed him the bottle. My job was done. I asked, he said no.

My mission was proceeding perfectly.

The Land of Mom bloomed with gingham and chintz and lots of flowery fabric I couldn't name.

Our house was a showroom. The downstairs furniture was gone, replaced by lines of false walls and windows all framed by Mom's curtains.

She had started a business. Curtains by Cookie. Mom's name was Lois, but it didn't sound right—"Curtains by Lois." Sounded like a failure. But "Curtains by Cookie," that was a winner.

Six days a week the house was a hive. The phones buzzed, the fax spewed, intensely rich women tiptoed around the false walls and murmured "Um-um-um" and "How do you do it?" and "I must have one" as they peered through the glassless windows.

I learned a whole new set of rituals, phone manners, a dialect of fabric and flattery. I practiced blending. I blended best near the beige corduroy. If I dared answer the phone, I always said Cookie was with a customer. I beamed when women raved about my mother's skill with scissors and a needle.

CookieMom nodded and smiled and snipped and sewed and phoned and sketched and delivered and installed. There was one tearful month when she tried to do all that and vacuum and cook and wash my shorts. Then we hired a cleaning lady and found the deli-ready section of the grocery store. The hardest part was convincing her I was old enough to do my own laundry.

The business almost kept her busy enough to forget about college. But not quite.

"Shouldn't you be hearing from those schools soon? Hand me those pins."

The basement was her workshop. My Ping-Pong table had been requisitioned for the cause. CookieMom pinned a pleat with mathematical precision.

"Joanna at the salon's daughter, she's going to Penn State." (*If that bubblehead got in, then they'll take you no matter what you got in chemistry.*)

I handed over the pins.

"Are you sure that purple stuff goes with the green, Mom? Looks kind of . . . loud." (*Please don't figure out the deadlines have all passed.*)

"Mrs. Hawkins wants to make a statement in her sunroom that will be unforgettable." (*Since when do you know from color?*)

"I have homework." (*Retreat!*)

"Your clothes are dry. I heard the buzzer."

Running away was the strategic alternative to being trapped in a lie. No, I hadn't applied to any colleges. No, I hadn't talked to Sergeant Payne about enlisting. I was waiting, suffering endless tours of duty with one parent, then the other. Waiting for the right envelope.

I dumped my laundry on the floor. My shorts were all pink. Why did that keep happening?

Mom had made my bed.

I was going to miss her.

I couldn't wait to leave.

The Kingdom of Dad was draped in black. Heather was no more.

The potential Queen-to-Bee had fled to the Kingdom of Howie.

137

Howie and Dad had played nine holes every Friday afternoon for seventeen years. King Howie had a cousin in L.A. who promised Heather a speaking part in a disaster movie. Good-bye fur coat.

The Kingdom of Dad was sending out black-edged press releases.

"She said she loved me."

"I gave her everything she wanted."

"Who am I going to play with on Fridays?"

He spent one day with a bottle of vodka and most of the night in the bathroom getting rid of it. The next morning I handed him a cup of coffee.

"We will never speak her name again." (*Please don't rub it in.*)

"Whose name?" (*I am so glad you aren't going to marry a girl three years older than me.*)

"That's my boy. And this thing." He waved vaguely at the coffee, his headache, the vodka bottle still on the table. (*You won't tell your mother how hard I took it, will you?*)

"Never happened." (*I don't have to say a word. She'll know as soon as she gets a look at you. I can't wait to get out of here.*)

He feigned a punch at my gut. I countered too fast and socked him hard in the shoulder. He wasn't expecting it. He staggered and swore. But his head hurt too much to yell at me.

Dad called an anonymous hot line and turned in Howie for cheating on his taxes. You should never piss off golfing buddies. He felt much better when he got off the phone. So good that he decided to get me in shape. Didn't want me to look like a wuss in boot camp.

We set out for a five-mile run and made it to the end of the block. Dad looked like one of those insurance commercials where the guy keels over of a heart attack and his widow has to beg on the street. Not a good sight.

He leaned against the lamppost.

"My knee," he said. "War wound."

As soon as he stopped moving he looked better. His problem was an extra sixty pounds around his gut.

I sympathized. "Knees are the worst." Always the diplomat.

It came while Dad was holding up the lamppost. A little white truck with blue and red stripes. The mail truck. Dad leaned on me and we limped home. I wanted to drop him, but that would not have been appropriate. Each step took an hour. It took all my training not to scream.

"I'll get the mail," I said. (*Put ice on your knee and go on a diet.*)

"Hunh." (*I better get some ice on this knee. Fried chicken for dinner sounds good. And ice cream.*)

He pulled himself up the stairs to the front door. I waited until the door closed behind him before I ripped open the envelope with my teeth.

The little blue book fit in my hand, soft as a girl's promise on a summer night. I opened it to see my grinning face and proof I was a citizen of the U.S. of A., followed by thick, empty pages. My permission slip out of this life, my Pass Go and Collect $200 card.

My missions to the Land of Mom and the Kingdom of Dad were over. I was finished with shuttle diplomacy. Rome called. Sydney beckoned. Tokyo lured. Nairobi invited.

My passport had arrived.

BY GRAHAM SALISBURY

Something Like . . . Love

"I telling you, he's the one. I know," Uncle Louie said. "Trouble is, I got no proof. That's what I need you for, the proof. You get me it, and I'll give you a reward. Go nose around the guy and see what you can see."

I squeezed the sponge over the side of the boat, then went back to wiping the salt off Uncle Louie's Penn Senator fishing reels.

"What kind of reward?" I said.

"Five bucks."

"*Pshhh.*"

"What do you mean, *Pshhh?*"

"Make it twenty and we can talk."

"*Twenty!*"

I shrugged. "Okay forget it, then." I didn't want the job, anyway. Who wanted to spy on somebody?

"You're more worse than the *crook.*"

140

"Fine. Who cares about your glass ball? It was just superstition, anyway."

Uncle Louie narrowed his eyes, like he was telling me, Listen here you ungrateful little rat.

His deckhand had just quit, and I was helping him clean up the boat after a morning charter. He wanted me to do it for free, but Dad said I should charge him two bucks, just on principle. Which got a frown out of Uncle Louie, whose way of thinking was: Hey, family is family, and should help each other, for free.

Right.

But I liked Uncle Louie, grouchy as he was. He was funny.

He bunched his lips and said, "Okay, okay, twenty bucks. Jesse. But you gotta get proof that he has it. *Proof.*"

He handed me the binoculars. "That's him over there."

I gave him the sponge.

He pointed across the bay, toward the old Hawaiian Palace Museum. "That's the guy. And it ain't just superstition. If I lose that glass ball, I don't catch no fish. Simple as that."

"What am I looking for?"

"You see that guy? The black guy?"

"Sitting on the grass?"

"That's him."

"Who is he?"

"How should I know? Just some bum."

The man looked like he was making something. I couldn't see what. I asked, "So how come you think he stole it?"

"Somebody saw him yesterday, checking out my boat when I was taking my charter back to the hotel. He was with a haole girl, a kid almost. Maybe he's a pimp." Louie humphed and mumbled. "That's all we need."

"Did you call the police?"

"Of course not. What they going care about a glass ball? I going take care of this myself."

The *Lady Jane* rocked gently alongside the pier, roasting in the afternoon sun. The harbor was blue-green and glassy, and the sky was for once completely clear of clouds, even up around the mountain. I gave the binoculars back to Uncle Louie.

"If he was going to steal something, why didn't he take your reels? Or those binoculars? Why would he take a glass ball?"

"To sell it, what else? It's rare, you know. How many you seen got water inside?"

"Yeah, but sell it for what? Five bucks? Ten? You can find those things in the ocean, or on the beach."

Louie shook his head and dropped the sponge into the bucket of fresh water on the deck. "Ca-ripes," he said. "Just go get me some proof." He made a fist and said, "Then I going get a couple of friends, and me and them going pay a visit to that guy's place, wherever that might be."

After I wiped that boat squeaky clean, Uncle Louie told me to stow his fishing gear in the hold, a place he could lock. He dipped his chin toward the coconut trees. "You get the proof, you get the money."

I nodded. "You got it."

I stowed the rigs and swashed a bucket of fresh water over the stern deck, then stood around waiting to get paid. That was the deal. Cash. Same day. Louie had a bad memory. I learned that from Dad, who sold gas to the boats, and who was Uncle Louie's brother-in-law.

"You owe me some money?" I finally said.

Louie looked over at me and said, "Oh yeah . . . heh-heh, forgot."

I jumped up onto the pier with two crumpled-up dollar bills in my pocket. Not bad for one hour of brainless work. But twenty, now that was *real* money.

———

The black man sat on the grass in the shade just above a small sand beach at the end of the seawall. Behind him, the old white, wood-sided museum slept in a grove of tall coconut trees.

The guy looked about fifty or sixty. Anyway, he had white hair. His fingers worked fast, weaving a green coconut hat for a couple of tourists who were watching him. He wore only an old, faded pair of kakhi shorts. He nodded as I walked up.

One of his eyes didn't move, the left one. The color of his right eye was almost black, but the one that didn't move was as green as a par-rotfish.

"You got to get de coconut leaf fresh," he explained to the tourists. "Dey bend easy, like rubber. Let dem sit in de sun so dey get warm and sof'."

When the funny-eyed man finished he smiled, huge and wide. "Ah," he said, pushing himself up and kicking the kinks out of his legs.

I took a step back. The guy was about a mile taller than me, maybe six-six, or something close to that. And the skin on his chest was tight, not loose and flabby like most old guys.

He placed the hat on the woman's head. "Something from de is-lands for de lady." He looked at the man and added, "Four dollars and she's yours."

The tourist gave him a five, then turned to me. "Would you mind taking a picture of us?"

The black man stood between them, smiling innocently, as if noth-ing in the world bothered him, and certainly not Uncle Louie's sparkling green, water-filled glass ball.

I took two pictures and the couple left.

"Like to see dem smile, eh?" the black man said, watching them walk away. He took a deep breath, then looked at me and said, "And what's your name, mon?"

"Kai."

"Ho, nice. Means ocean, right?"

I nodded, then said, "Who are you and what are you doing here?" *Jeez, what am I, crazy? I was supposed to be a spy, for cripes sake.*

The man laughed, a loud and full sound that made me smile. "I am Jukka. From de Cays, mon. You know where's de Cays?"

I shook my head, trying not to look at the green eye.

"Glass," he said, pointing to the weird eye. "Got poked out with a stick. In de Cays. Mon with lizard boots. Sit, boy."

I sat cross-legged on the grass, and the man, Jukka, made a couple of slits in a palm frond with a small knife, then laid the knife on the grass, a single-blade pocket knife with a white handle. I asked if I could look at it.

"You like dat?" he said. "Whale bone. Got it from my daddy when I was a boy, like you. Bes' knife I ever had."

I picked up the knife and ran my fingers over the well-worn handle, then tested the cutting edge with my thumb. I folded it, and opened it, then folded it again. "Nice," I said.

Jukka smiled. "Dat it is, mon. Say, you know where a mon could get some mackerel?"

I turned and pointed toward the small grocery store across the street. "We call them opelu."

"Yah, mon, I know where to buy dem. But can I get dem fresh? Alive?"

"Catch them."

He laughed again and said he had to make a living and didn't have time for fishing. "I give you fifty cents for each fish you bring me, dat is, if you want de business."

Whoa, I was being offered money by the bucket these days. I shrugged. It might be a lot of work for fifty cents a fish.

"I'll think about it."

Jukka said, "Good mon, you think about it," and tied up his palm

144

fronds and hung them over his shoulder on a string. Then he got this ratty old red Honda-90 motorbike out from behind some garbage cans by the museum and putted away, his knees pointing out to the sides like wings. He vanished around the corner, turning up toward the mountain, away from the crowd on the pier.

When I told Uncle Louie that I'd met the black man, he said, "Good, good. Now find out where's his place."

I could just see it, Louie and his bomboola friends creeping up on some poor old cardboard shack on the beach. Made me nervous. I liked the black man.

Opelu ran during the winter months, mostly. Not summer. But still, you could catch them. I thought hard about the fifty cents a fish. And the twenty bucks. And the two dollars I got every time I scrubbed down Uncle Louie's boat. I could get rich.

"Okay," I told Jukka the next day. "I'll work for you. How many fish you want me to get?"

Jukka rubbed his chin, sunspots reflecting off his green eye. "Oh, bucket of twenty or so," he said. "Dat should be fine. Twenty fish every day."

My eyes must have popped when he said twenty fish a *day*. He laughed and ran his big hand over my head. "Can you do it?"

"S . . . sure I can do it . . . no problem."

For the next week, while Louie was out fishing, I used his skiff to catch Jukka's opelu.

At that time of year I had the ocean to myself. On a good day I caught twenty fish in a matter of minutes. And on a bad one I was lucky to pull in half that many in a couple of hours. I used hand lines in a hundred feet of water, five hooks on each line, three feet apart, and a lead sinker at the bottom. Why did Jukka want live opelu, anyway? Did he eat them? Twenty a day?

So I asked.

And Jukka said, "She gotta eat, eh?"

"Who's gotta eat?"

Jukka smiled and wagged a finger at me. "Dat, mon, is a secret."

One day, after Jukka had taken off on his motorbike with his palm fronds and bucket of fish, I got this great idea: follow him. Uncle Louie would love that.

But Jukka had that motorbike.

I needed wheels.

Uncle Louie had them.

He squinted at me from the deck of his boat. He liked the idea of me following Jukka, but not the part about letting me use his brand new motorcycle, a Kawasaki 500, which he kept in his garage under a tarp.

"Tomorrow," I said. "I'll follow him when he goes home."

"Tst," he finally spit. "Okay, okay, use 'um."

To him, that glass ball was his *lifeline,* I tell you. Fishermen are *so* superstitious. "But you bust that bike, you going to pay . . . or your daddy going to pay," he said.

"Don't worry, old man. I can handle it."

"Hey! Don't old man me or I slap your head."

I grinned.

Uncle Louie scowled. When I started away, he called, "Hey! *Nail* 'um."

The next day I got an early start on fishing. I got lucky and caught twenty fish by eleven o'clock, then headed straight for Uncle Louie's house.

I lugged the Kawasaki out of the garage, snappy red with lots of shiny chrome. *Vrrroooom!* The sound was huge. It idled like a purring cat and took off like a rocket. This was turning out to be one *great* summer.

I beat Jukka to the museum by a half hour and had plenty of time

146

to hide the motorcycle. By the time he came puttering in, I was lying on the grass under the coconut trees.

The afternoon clouds were beginning to roll down from the mountain, slow as slugs. I wondered what Jukka would if he caught me following him.

He walked up and handed me the empty bucket from the day before. I sat up and pointed to the full one. He took it to a shady spot near his motorbike.

"Beautiful day, eh?" he said, easing down next to me.

I nodded, thinking Jukka would have said it was a beautiful day even if a hurricane had been passing through. That's the kind of guy he was. Always happy. He didn't seem like any thief to me.

Jukka peeled two five-dollar bills off a good-sized wad and paid me. Then he started in on a hat. I wondered where he'd gotten all that money.

"Can't make much money making hats," I said.

"Ah, dat's true, dat's true. But dat's also not de first thing you look at. No, mon."

"When I get out of school, I'm gonna get a charter fishing boat, like my uncle. You know his boat? The *Lady Jane*? Ever seen it?"

"*Lady Jane* . . . no, I don't think so."

I studied him a moment, then said, "Well anyway, these waters are the best in the world for marlin fishing."

"Maybe so, mon. Leas' till you been to de Gulf Stream."

"I don't know about any stream, but wherever it is it ain't as good as the ocean."

Jukka laughed and put down his knife. "Dass good, mon. Dass good."

"So what's the first thing you look at, if not the money?"

"Dere's only one thing dat means something, boy, and dat is dat you spen' your life in your own way."

"And *this* is your way?" I pointed my chin at the emerging hat in Jukka's hands.

"I'm free, mon. I go where I want, I do what I want. I don't need money. 'Cept to eat."

"Don't you want a house, or something? A place to live like everyone else?"

"I got a place to live."

"Where?"

"Here," Jukka said, tapping his heart.

When the boats started coming in, Jukka packed up his stuff and buzzed away, the motorbike smoking like a dump fire. The second he was out of sight, I sprinted across the street and started up the Kawasaki.

I raced around the bend where I'd last seen him. He was nowhere in sight. The road went two ways: up the mountain, or north along the coast. I took the coast.

When I zipped around the first bend in the hot old potholed two-lane, I almost ran up Jukka's tailpipe. I hit the brakes, swerved to a stop, and nearly went over the handlebars.

"Jeez!" I said.

But Jukka didn't hear me, just kept on going, his motorbike smoking and making such a racket that he didn't even know I was there.

That part of the coast, and for miles beyond, was pretty much all lava rock, acres and acres of old volcanic flows with very little of anything growing. Keeping out of sight wasn't going to be easy, but at least I could see Jukka from a distance. I crept after him.

About a quarter mile later, he left the road and headed out over the lava, following an old Jeep trail. Hanging on a rusty chain across the trail was a sign that said, KEEP OUT—PRIVATE PROPERTY. But Jukka just went on around it.

I waited, gave Jukka some distance, then went on.

After about ten minutes of jerking and twisting over the uneven rock, I came to a green grove at the edge of the sea, a place that had been spared by the old lava flows. The road dropped down into a thicket of dry keawe trees and weedy underbrush.

I turned off the engine and coasted to a stop.

I hid the motorcycle and started down the trail. I couldn't see the ocean yet, or even hear any waves, but the air smelled like salt. It was kind of spooky.

A dog suddenly started barking, getting louder and louder, coming my way. In seconds, a German Shepherd burst out in front of me, snarling and showing teeth.

I sprinted for the nearest tree, just barely making it. The dog sounded like it wanted to rip my heart out.

"*Ssssst,*" someone hissed, and the dog shut up and started whining, but kept its eyes on me.

Somebody laughed.

"I wondered when you would show up out here," Jukka said. "If a boy ain't got curiosity, den he not much a boy." Jukka caught the dog by its collar. "De puppy won't bite, 'less I tell him to. Come on out of de tree."

I inched down. I didn't like the way the dog was watching me. I let him come up and sniff my hand. He shoved at it with his snotty nose, wagging his tail as if he hadn't wanted to chew me to shreds only a minute earlier.

"Now listen, mon. You got to know de secret ol' Jukka been keeping', dass why you here. Okay. I show you. But firs' you tell me you don' tell nobody what you seein' here today." He gave me a serious look with his good eye.

"I won't tell anybody," I said. "Promise."

"Good. Follow me."

The dry brush and trees gave way to thick, green clumps of grass that bent inland. The road turned from rock to sand and ended at the marshy edge of a wide, glass-clear lagoon. Grassy islands and dark waterways disappeared under overhanging trees on the far side. On the sea side, a mounded sand and grass spit of land hid the lagoon from the ocean.

In front of us, at the edge of the lagoon, and built out over it on stilt-legs, was a sagging gray-wood, tin-roof fisherman's shack. Jukka's dog trotted over to it and settled down in the shade.

In the corner of my eye I thought I saw something move, something in the lagoon. Over near one of the grassy islands. I turned, but nothing was there.

Jukka swept his hand toward the doorless shack, saying, "Come inside, mon."

The rusty roof was held up by three walls, with the far side open to the lagoon. I tested my footing before going inside, thinking the place might come down around me if I moved too fast.

Jukka laughed. "Don't worry, she's stronger than she looks."

On the floor of the one-room shack were two foam mattresses, each with a sleeping bag on it. An old wood pier ran out into the water, right from the back side of the shack. A small cooler and some grocery bags stood against one of the walls, and out where the pier started, a five-gallon bottle of water glinted in the sun.

There was no glass ball anywhere in sight.

But . . . there were *two* mattresses.

"Not much, mon, but dis is where I sleep. Sometimes I get tired of de rockin' boat."

"What rocking boat?

"In de bay. Come."

I followed him back outside. He pointed to two masts sticking up above the sandy spit. "Dass my real home. You want to see it?"

"Yeah, sure."

150

Jukka walked ahead, out over the spit to the ocean side, where a sandy beach curved along the shore. Small round pebbles rattled in the easy shore break. An old beat-up skiff was staked in the sand several feet above the water line.

"Dere she is, boy," Jukka said, gazing out into the bay.

The sailboat, like the skiff, was definitely tired. It rolled gently in the low swells, bow to the sea. A second anchor line ran off its stern. The letters across the transom read, AURORE, BIMINI.

"Dat's where I live," Jukka said.

"I thought you said you lived in here," I said, tapping my heart.

Jukka thought that was hilarious. "You very funny, mon, you know that? Come. De secret is in de pond."

We went back to the shack and through it to the pier that jutted out into the lagoon from its far side. The water there was blue-black, ice-clear, and glassy. A coolness rose off its surface. The place smelled sweet, like rust and mud.

Again, there was a movement in the near distance.

But this time, I saw something.

Holy *moly*.

Jukka saw me gawking, then called out, "Star!"

As she rose from the water I nearly stopped breathing.

My eyes about popped out of my head. She stood watching us, motionless. A girl, knee-deep in a tidal pool at the edge of the lagoon, as naked as a peeled banana. Ai-yah!

I guess she was about eighteen or nineteen, somewhere around there. A couple years older than me, anyway. Took me about two seconds to fall in love. Okay, so maybe it wasn't *love*, but it sure was part of what love is made up of, I know that much.

The girl said nothing. She didn't wave or smile or even try to cover herself.

"*That's* the secret?" I asked.

151

Jukka laughed, then more soberly said, "No. That one is a lost child." He gazed a moment at her, then added, "I foun' her in de Abacos, drifting in Marsh Harbor. She don't talk now—drugs almos' kill her. She come down from de States. When I foun' her she was barely human. She would steal the shirt right off your back. But she don't do it now. No, she jus' need somebody to care, eh?"

Jukka watched the girl a moment longer, his good eye soft and full of something like love, or sadness. Hard to tell.

The girl turned away and vanished into the trees.

Jukka sighed. "Sit, mon. I show you de secret."

He went back into the shack and came out with a polished silver flute that cast jiggling sun spots over the pier. He played a couple of notes as he walked toward me. "De magic flute," he said, his white teeth gleaming in the sun.

This was getting to be one strange day.

Jukka sat down next to me and slipped his feet into the water. The girl was out of sight now, somewhere in the trees.

Jukka put the flute under his lower lip and began to play, soft, breathy, and crisp in the still lagoon.

As he played he pointed out into the water with his chin.

What? I couldn't see anything. Then I spotted a dark V-shaped set of ripples on the surface, moving toward us. Then a fin, like a shark. I pulled my feet up.

Jukka stopped playing and put the flute down, then clapped his hands together.

In that instant a gray porpoise, five or six feet long, flew out of the water, almost stopped at the top of a flawless arc, then fell and disappeared beneath the surface.

"De secret, mon."

"A porpoise?" I said.

"Dolphin. I train her. Not too long I have her doing tricks. She swim with me, jump when I say jump. I bring de tourists down here. Dolphin very smart, smarter den dogs. Maybe Jukka got a new business, eh?"

I gaped at him, like, Are you *serious?* Nobody was going to come down here. It was private property. If anybody *did* come it would be to kick Jukka out of there.

Jukka laughed and patted me on the back. "You will see, mon. You will see."

He went on to tell me about how he and the girl had caught the porpoise with a net while they were sailing off the coast.

"De dolphin can take your leg off, mon," he said. "Or she can beat you dead with her fluke, dass what dey call de tail. But she don't. Dey like people. In all de history of de world dey friends with humans."

Jukka slipped into the chest-deep water and asked me to go get the bucket of fish. "I mostly feed her in the evening," he said. "But as you are here, now will be fine."

I ran out, found the bucket of opelu, and started back through the shack. But I stopped, remembering why I'd come there. It would only take a second.

I checked the pier. Jukka was swimming. I put the bucket down and felt around the two mattresses. No glass ball. Maybe it was in the box of clothes.

When I bent over the box I got the shock of my life—a pair of feet. Standing next to me.

"Uh . . ."

The girl.

She'd wrapped a length of red material around her like a sarong, and tucked in a bunch near her shoulder to hold it in place. Her skin was tanned the color of a sunburned gourd. Her eyes stabbed into me like ice picks.

I stood and backed away. "I . . . was looking for . . . Jukka's knife."

She waited. Piercing eyes. Cold eyes.

I picked up the bucket, sloshing the water.

The girl, Star, didn't even blink.

I left quickly, my hands trembling from getting caught like that. I didn't look back but I knew she was still watching me. I could feel it on the back of my neck.

Back out on the pier, Jukka reached up to the bucket and pulled out an opelu, alive, but not by very much. I took a deep breath and tried to settle down.

The porpoise came up to us and stuck its head out of the water. It had a kind of smile on its face. I'd seen hundreds of them out on the marlin grounds, but never like that. Never *smiling*.

But who cared? All I wanted was for my hands to stop shaking. The girl was so cold. And so . . . so beautiful, in a kind of dangerous way. Gave me the chills.

Jukka tossed the opelu into the water, and the porpoise chased it down instantly. "Best to feed dem live fish so dey don't forget how to catch dere own food."

"What?"

Jukka looked at me and said, "Jump in de water, mon. Feel de skin. Don't worry, she good, friendly animal."

I slid off the pier into the cool, silky lagoon, which for me was about neck deep. The bottom was muddy sand. The porpoise shot away, but circled back and nosed between me and Jukka. I put my hand on its skin and felt the tension, the power.

"Feels weird to be treating a fish like a pet," I said.

"Not a fish, mon. Animal. Go under. Watch her move."

I dropped under. It was blurry, but I could still see the porpoise swim by, right in front of me. Its skin rippled as it moved. It was a powerful sight, all right.

But not as powerful as Star's ice-pick eyes.

Later, when I told Louie what I'd found, he rubbed his chin and thought for a minute, then mumbled, "I should have him arrested for trespassing. No, no. Not yet. First you got to get on that boat. Check it out."

"What?"

"That's prob'ly where he keeps what he steals."

This whole thing about Jukka and Uncle Louie's good-luck glass ball was beginning to sour me. It was just a glass float, for cripes sake. What was the big deal? Sure he was superstitious, sure he thought it brought him good luck, but so what? Anyway, I couldn't believe that Jukka would steal anything. Look at what he was doing for the girl. He'd saved her *life*.

When I told Uncle Louie I thought he was wrong, he told me I was too green to understand about these bums. He knew. He'd seen it all before.

The next day when I showed up at the museum with a fresh bucket of fish, Jukka wasn't there. I sat and waited.

Almost ten minutes passed before I noticed the *Aurore* across the bay, tied alongside the pier. I got up and walked over to it.

"De boat needed gas," Jukka said.

"If you bought gas, it was from my dad."

"Ah, now I see," Jukka said. "Nice daddy, nice boy."

Star poked her head out of the cabin companionway. She hesitated when she saw me on the pier. Jukka motioned her out saying, "Come, come," but she didn't move.

She stared at me, and waited.

155

"She needs to see de town," Jukka said. "She been too long without peoples." Star disappeared back into the cabin.

"Where's the dog?"

"Back at de place."

I nodded and checked out the *Aurore*, its wood deck and silver wheel, its confusion of cables and neatly stowed sails. I wondered how I could get myself invited aboard. That's what Uncle Louie wanted, wasn't it? I kind of wanted it, myself. But for different reasons.

"Don't see many sailboats around here," I said. "Only fishing boats, and sometimes a Coast Guard cutter or the Navy."

"You like to take a ride?"

"Really?"

"We going to anchor in de harbor for de night, but I don't mind sailing down de coast a ways. Plenty daylight left."

"Well, sure, *yeah*."

"Get on board, mon."

Took me less than a second. Uncle Louie would be proud.

"Star," Jukka called. "We're going for a ride."

Star finally emerged from the cabin and scurried around the deck, amazing me with her skill at hitching and unhitching an octopus of ropes and cables. Jukka started up the engine. It coughed and spit. He stood at the wheel, guiding the boat out of the harbor under diesel power. Smoke clouded out from the exhaust vent. The engine vibrated in the floorboards. And Star scrambled about the deck without a word of direction from Jukka.

"She know de boat," Jukka shouted over the racket of the old engine.

About ten minutes out, Jukka and Star unfurled the sails and shut the engine down. The wind was mild, but strong enough.

And I entered a whole new world.

Never in my life had I been on a sailboat. Only canoes, skiffs, and fishing boats.

Now, there was no droning engine, no smell of fuel, just the quiet *shhhhhhh* of a bow cutting water, and the thumping hull, rising and falling. Jukka clanged a brass bell near the wheel. I turned to look. He tapped his heart and grinned.

A few minutes later he called to me. "Come." He waved me to the cockpit. "Take the wheel. Jus' hold her easy. She good, strong boat."

I clenched the chrome handgrips, trying to hold to a steady course. The quiet, watery vibrations hummed through my fingers as the *Aurore* sliced the sea.

"What de whole world needs is one day at de wheel of a good, easy, sailing boat," Jukka said.

I guessed he was right about that. Oh, *man*, was it nice—the salty smell of the sea breezing over my shirtless body, the hum of the keel in my fingers and feet, the hush of the rushing sea, the muscle of the wind snapping the sail taut, the thrilling tilt of the deck. I'd never felt anything like it before. Not even close.

"In all of my life I am most happy when I am sitting at de wheel, just like you are, with de wind in my face and dreams in my head."

This is heaven, I thought. No, *more* than heaven.

Minutes later, with me still at the wheel, and Jukka standing behind me, Star peeked up from the companionway. How'd she do that? I hadn't even seen her go in. She glanced at us, and her gaze lingered a moment. But now, in her eyes, there was something new. A small flicker of life, or some kind of faraway hope. Of something, anyway. Something new.

Then I saw it.

Cradled in her hands, the water-filled glass ball.

She held it tenderly, as if it were a kitten, or a puppy.

Jukka put a hand on my shoulder and said, "Nice, eh?" Meaning the glass ball. "She found it on de beach."

Star held it up and looked into it to see the water sloshing inside, clear and green and amazing. The faintest smile tugged at her eyes, and for the first time I saw a warmth in them.

"It is the firs' thing to bring her happiness in a long, long time, boy."

I had no words to say.

Not one.

The next day dawned clear and warm.

I went down to the harbor to watch the fishing boats set out, then take Uncle Louie's skiff out for Jukka's opelu. Uncle Louie's boat was tied up at the pier, getting ready.

"Your friend is in trouble," Louie said. "The police are looking for him."

"Who? Jukka?"

"That's the guy's name?"

"If you mean the guy I been watching."

"Yeah him. Last night I was in Ocean View for dinner," Louie said, "and him and the haole girl came in. They sat near the door, just a couple of tables from the entrance to the bar area. You couldn't help but notice them, the guy so big and the girl wearing shorts and half a T-shirt. Hoo, look nice.

"Anyway, there were a couple of drunk guys in the bar, yeah? And they saw the girl and came out to get a closer look. I don't know what they said to her, or to the big guy, but one of the drunk guys put his hand on the girl's shoulder, and the girl started screaming.

"*Ho,* I never seen somebody move fast as that black man. *Boom!* He was on top of the drunk guy, punching him, *pow, pow!* Then the drunk guy pulled out a knife, but the black man took it away. Somehow the drunk guy got cut on the arm. Shee, blood everywhere." Louie winced at the memory of it. "Must have hurt like hell."

Then Louie shook his head and said, "The drunk guy yelled, 'He cut me! He cut me!' and the girl was still screaming, and the black guy grabbed her, and the two of them took off running. I told you he was trouble," Louie said. "I told you."

As soon as Louie headed out of the harbor, I raced up to his house and got out his motorcycle. By nine o'clock I was skirting around the KEEP OUT sign and heading down the trail to Jukka's lagoon.

The place was deserted.

I ran out to the sandy pit. No skiff, no sailboat. A quiet breeze blew inland over the flat sea, but otherwise the place was as still as a bucket of water.

Gone.

I picked up a stone to throw out to sea, but dropped it and looked back at the lagoon. "Hey," I said out loud. "What about the porpoise?"

I raced through the shack and out onto the pier. I slapped my hands together. Nothing. I tried again.

Maybe I needed something louder.

I ran into the shack and found a couple of loose boards to slap together.

Just as I was about to go back out, I saw Jukka's whalebone pocket-knife stuck into the wall. Below the blade the letter *K* was carved into the wood.

K for what? Kai? What else could it be?

I pulled the knife out and folded it. How could he leave this, the one he said he'd had since his daddy gave it to him when he was a boy? I put the knife in my pocket.

Back out on the pier I managed a crisp crack with the boards that echoed out over the lagoon like a rifle shot.

An arrow of ripples spread on the water. I clapped the boards again, and the porpoise came up and circled around below me.

"I gotta get you out of here," I said. "Or you'll starve."

How could Jukka just leave her in here like that? Maybe he couldn't get her out. Maybe he was in too much of a hurry. I mean, he did cut a guy.

I went back to the sandy pit and followed it along the shoreline until I found the inlet to the lagoon. It was a small opening, and with the tide out, far too shallow for the porpoise to escape.

To keep the porpoise in the lagoon during high tide Jukka had stretched some chicken wire across the channel. Now the wire was lying flat on the sand beneath about a foot and a half of water. Looked like he'd tried to get her out, anyway.

I turned toward the ocean. I'd have to wait for high tide to chase her out.

The tide came in just after sunset, slowly, steadily. The ocean surged into the channel in foamy swirls of clear salt water. But it was after dusk before it was deep enough.

I didn't know how to chase her out, only to call her. So I took the boards out into the ocean, waded out up to my chest and raised the boards over my head. I slapped them together, over and over and over, until my arms nearly fell off.

I must have been slapping them together for a half hour before the porpoise got the message and headed toward the sea. I caught a glimpse of her fin in the darkening water, and felt her whiz past me. "Good luck," I whispered.

I dragged myself ashore and lay down on the still-warm sand. A billion stars sparkled across the sky above.

Stars.

All so peaceful above.

It was in that moment that I thought of Star, thought of her on the *Aurore,* coming up the companionway with Uncle Louie's good-luck glass ball. And the look in her eyes as she cradled it.

The peace in them. The smallest hint of life.

The moon rose behind the mountain, wispy clouds ringing it with the colors of the rainbow.

And it all fell into place.

Yes.

The knife was a . . . a prize . . . a prize for a prize.

A *trade,* is what it was.

Of course. Jukka knew all along where that ball had come from. The knife wasn't a gift to me, but to Star. He gave me his most prized possession for my silence. That was it. He did it for Star, who had nothing and nobody in this whole entire world but a dreamy old man and a stolen glass ball with water in it that almost made her life worth living.

I fingered the knife in my pocket, suddenly wondering if I was wrong and Jukka wanted me to give it to Uncle Louie to make up for his loss. Me or Uncle Louie, it didn't really matter. I didn't want to give it to him. But I probably would, even though the complaining old shark didn't deserve it. But then he *did* give something up for somebody other than himself. Even if he didn't know it. But the glass ball would be my secret forever.

I creaked up with tired and rubbery bones, still thinking about Jukka. "It's a deal," I whispered.

Our agreement slowly anchored itself somewhere deep inside me. It was right and I knew it. I knew it because it made me feel something . . . something new, something big, something good. Really good.

Something like . . . love.

BY CHRIS CRUTCHER

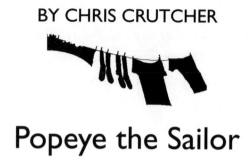

Popeye the Sailor

From Johnny Barker's File—1981:

Johnny: I had this brother.

Wilson: Oh, yeah? Older or younger?

Johnny: Younger. (Looks at the floor) He's not around no more. He's not alive.

Wilson: Oh. What happened?

Johnny: He sort of popped.

Wilson: Your brother popped?

Johnny: We was teachin' 'im not to pee.

Wilson: You and your mother?

Johnny: Yeah, only she was makin' me do it.

Wilson: Making you do what?

Johnny: Teach 'im. She was makin' me fill him up with water. You know, teach 'im a lesson.

Wilson: How old were you?

Johnny: (Shrugs) I dunno. Little.

Wilson: Tell me what happened.

Johnny: (Very tentative) He peed, an' mom was sick of it. She been tellin' him he better cut it out an' he peed right after she said it, so she got this blanket only it wasn't like a real blanket, it was like all slick.

Wilson: A rubber sheet?

Johnny: Yeah, like that. An' she puts it down on the rug an' sits Edgar on it an' gives 'im this bottle of water to drink, like she's gonna teach 'im to hold it. His pee, I mean. An' he drinks an' she makes me go fill it up an' give it to 'im, an' when he don't want the rest she slaps him on the side of the head an' says drink it, an' when he don't she starts screamin'. An' he finally drinks it an' she sends me for another one, only now she makes me be the one to hit 'im if he won't drink. At first I don't want to, but she says it's for him . . . that it will make him a better kid an' that sometimes you got to do things that seem mean to make a good kid. So I starts hittin' him an' makin' him drink it, an' it gets harder an' harder to do 'cause he don't want it no more, but finally every time he goes ahead. An' my mom is screamin' at him he better not go to the bathroom or she's gonna snatch 'im bald-headed, an' pretty soon I give 'im the bottle again, an' slap him a good one an' his head kinda falls over to the side an' a big ol' buncha pee gets in a puddle around 'im an' his eyes are open, but he ain't seein' nothin', an' all of a sudden my mom is screamin' at me that I killed 'im, an' screamin' in the telephone an' then the hospital people are comin' an' she hides the rubber thingy an' tells me don't say nothin' about what happened or I'll have to go to jail. An' that was it. Edgar never come home from the hospital.

Wilson: And you think you killed him?

Johnny:	I know I done it. They come an' took me away.
Wilson:	You ever see your mother again, Johnny?
Johnny:	Yup. At the social worker place. But I never got to go live at our house again.
Wilson:	That's because your mother couldn't take care of you, Johnny. See, when you're that little and your mother makes you do something, you kind of have to do it. So it's her fault about your brother, not yours.
Johnny:	Could we play with Popeye some more?

Note: Checked client's story against Child Protection Service records. Generally checks out. Younger brother, Edgar, appeared at Sacred Heart Hospital in a coma with internal injuries. Mother blamed older brother. Child removed, placed in foster-adopt home. Parental rights eventually terminated. —Wilson Corder.

Fall 1997

Johnny Barker walks down the hall, fingers gently but firmly wrapped around four-year-old Alex's ankles, which are draped over his shoulders. Alex holds tight to Johnny's forehead, issuing orders. "Drink!" he demands, and Johnny grips a little tighter, bends at the waist, bringing Alex close to the drinking fountain.

"Turn it," Alex tells him.

"You turn it," Johnny says back.

"Who's the boss?" Alex asks, parroting the name of the game they're playing.

"You're the boss," Johnny says, "but if I let go of your legs to turn the handle, you're toast."

A hesitation. It makes perfect four-year-old sense, and Alex tentatively releases one hand from Johnny's forehead, gripping tighter with his tiny arm, and turns the handle. More water drips down his chin than reaches his mouth, but he pats Johnny's head and Johnny straightens up. "Back to the classroom," Johnny says.

"No!" Alex yells. "There." he points to the far end of the hall.

"Back to the classroom," Johnny says again. "Your horse's shoulders are killing him. How much do you weigh anyway?"

"C'mon. One more time."

"Later," Johnny says, and heads toward the classroom door, stopping before the open entrance. "What's inside a sleeping bag?" he asks, to which Alex replies, "Duck down," and does, avoiding a bump on his head.

Kevin pushes a book he wants read in Johnny's face as Alex slides from his shoulders to the windowsill. Carey jumps up, arms outstretched, wanting a ride. Jerry begs to build a jail for his mom's boyfriend. All are four years old. Johnny walks to the clock, showing each where the hands will be when it's their turn, then sells them on joining what he'll be doing between now and then. He takes the book from Kevin, and the children sit in a tight circle.

Katherine, the head therapist for Community Mental Health's child abuse project, looks up from drawing pictures with Tara, a three-and-a-half-year-old long-term molestation victim, admiring the scene. Johnny's practicum here at the center has been a godsend.

As the last child leaves with his caseworker, Katherine says, "We're going to miss you around here, Johnny. Two more weeks. I finished your letter of recommendation. I'll send it to your advisor."

He thanks her.

"I don't know what we'll do without you," she says. "The kids are used to having you around, and so am I. I think you'll be a big name in this business someday."

Johnny thanks her again and pulls on his coat. Though his college quarter ends today, he is working in the abuse project through the break. "I got more than you got," he says honestly. "And more than the kids got. I don't know how I can thank you."

Katherine puts a hand on his shoulder softly. "Just go out there and do your magic," she says. "That's how you can thank us. Or better yet, come back here and work after you get your degree."

Johnny nearly reaches the outer exit when he stops, retraces his steps. From the classroom doorway he says, "Look, just because I'm not getting credits doesn't mean I have to stop. Can't I just volunteer?"

Katherine looks up in surprise. "Of course you can volunteer, but what about your studies?"

"I can schedule classes after noon," he tells her. "Might have to leave a half hour early or so, but I could cover most of the morning at least."

"You've already told the kids you're leaving."

"I'll un-tell them."

Katherine mounts an ingenuous protest, but Johnny calls over his shoulder, "It's a done deal."

Johnny sits just inside the door in Wilson's tiny office.

"So, in two weeks you're outta there," Wilson says.

"Not exactly."

"What is this, a Hertz commercial?"

"I'm going to volunteer. I can schedule next quarter's classes in the afternoon. But I still need your letter of recommendation before the end of this quarter."

Wilson leans back in his chair, placing the heels of his Reeboks on the desktop, and sighs.

"You think that's a bad idea, to volunteer?"

"I thought we agreed you needed to learn to leave things; how to go on. Remember, 'I get so stuck sometimes, Wilson'?"

"I know, but . . ."

"This isn't about those kids, Johnny."

Johnny looks away.

"Uh, Johnny Barker, right?" Wilson says. "Remember me, Wilson Corder? Your therapist? The guy you hired to help you through the thick deep brown stuff?"

"You mad at me?"

Wilson takes a deep breath. "No. I go home at night to my wonderful girlfriend and her two wonderful kids and their three wonderful dogs and two wonderful cats. You're the guy who lives with your decisions, not I."

"You think I should just leave." It is not a question.

"You're the guy who told me that, Johnny. Last week. What's this about?"

Johnny stands up, walks to the window overlooking the parking lot. "I don't know; those kids. Katherine . . ."

"Johnny, I've known Katherine Jaeger for almost twenty years. She could run that program by herself with one hand tied to the opposite foot." It's an exaggeration, but not by much.

"Then why didn't she protest when I said I'd stay?"

"Because free lunch doesn't come by often. Because I respect your confidentiality and haven't told her you're a compulsive maniac. Now what's this about?"

"What's it always about," Johnny says. "It's about what I owe."

Wilson stands, opens the door.

"You kicking me out?"

"It's an idea, but no. Follow me."

In the parking lot they stand next to a gleaming Honda 1100 Shadow motorcycle.

Johnny laughs. "You gonna give me this if I succeed in therapy?"

"In your dreams, buddy. You know how much this thing cost me?"

167

Johnny looks the bike over. He's admired it a lot, even ridden on it a time or two. He knows how much it cost. He says, "Eight thousand and change," quoting Wilson.

"Eight thousand and change," Wilson repeats. "Only it's actually more than that. Know why?"

"Tax?" Johnny guesses.

"And interest. Takes it close to twelve."

"There's a point here," Johnny says.

"Yes, there is a point. Every month I write out a check for a little more than two hundred dollars. First I pay off the interest; that's the way these bandits at the bank operate. Then I pay off the principal and tax. Then you know what?"

"What?"

"Then it's mine!" Wilson yells. *"Then I own it!"* From across the parking lot people stop, stare. Wilson waves to them. *"This is my bike,"* he yells to them. *"Two more payments and I own it!"* They look, walk on nervously.

Johnny says, "It's not the same."

"It's exactly the same, Johnny," Wilson says. "Only I know what mine cost and you don't. You're not willing to put a price on your guilt and pay the goddam thing off and get the hell on with your life, and if you don't it will never be paid for. You came back to me a year ago and said you wanted to be a therapist, that you were about to finish your undergraduate work."

"And you were skeptical."

"Do you remember why?"

"You said shit rolls downhill."

"And . . ."

"And if the shit in my life is going to stop, I'm going to have to stop it."

"And what is the shit, Johnny?"

168

"Being mean; anger."

"Naw, that's not the shit. The shit is guilt. The shit is shame. The shit is self-hate. Being mean is the *smell* of the shit. Get rid of the shit and there is no smell."

"So what do I do?"

"You figure it out."

"This is Johnny's last week," Katherine tells the class.

Alex glances toward Johnny in panic; Johnny glances back, a picture of apology.

He starts to say he'll come back and visit, but Katherine stops him with a firm, gentle look. It is no help to let abandoned kids look forward to something that may not happen. The world is better taken in its true light.

Alex returns from a trip to the bathroom and surveys the room. Jessica, blind in one eye from a blow to the head and tentative as a mouse three times trapped, plays with her back to him, dressing a doll in as many layers of clothing as she can get on her, protecting her from what happens if she's ever caught naked. Jessica never sees Alex coming. In a split second, Alex's fingers are entwined in her hair in a way that could earn him a knot-tying merit badge. Jessica's scream pierces the normal low din of the room, and Johnny, a classroom teacher, and an aide descend on the two. Johnny grips Alex's wrist, holds it close to Jessica's head so Alex can't pull, while the others unwind the hair and fingers. Alex struggles to keep a fist, while Johnny struggles to open it without hurting him. Three minutes later Jessica is free, crying softly, asking to be held. Katherine and Johnny are in the corner with Alex.

"You're mad," Katherine says.

Alex glares.

"I'd be mad if my friend was leaving, too."

169

Alex casts a hateful glance at Johnny, says nothing.

"I'll leave you two alone," she says. "Maybe you can find a way to talk to him about it, or something fun to play."

Alex walks away. "Stay close and don't push him," Katherine tells Johnny. "Just be available." She puts a gentle hand on Johnny's shoulder. Johnny's eyes brim with tears. "It's okay, Johnny. This is good for both of you. You have to let him work through it. We lose things."

Another scream pierces the room, and again the staff descends on Alex, this time performing the Houdini Hair Escape on Misty. For the first time Johnny is conscious of heat in his chest; anger rising. It scares him, and he pushes it back, calling it something else. There is blood on Misty's scalp and beneath Alex's nails.

Johnny increases his vigilance and Alex increases his stealth, waiting for that split second when Johnny's attention strays momentarily toward another kid before mounting another blitzkrieg on another unsuspecting victim; always someone defenseless. In each new attempt, Johnny catches him in the nick of time.

But inside it builds, that sense of incompetence, that failure to help Alex *understand* and protect the others. If he is not a protector, what is he? Anxiety and doubt begin to crowd out his intellect.

Most of the children have followed Katherine outside. A few remain, listening to a story read by an aide. As much for himself as for Alex, Johnny takes him to the back of the room to pummel the heavy bag mounted from the ceiling in the far corner. Alex shouts the names of his life's tormentors, delivering blows of enormous impact for a five-year-old, now and then sneaking in Johnny's name. "Get the Boffos," he demands, and Johnny turns for the padded foam clubs with which Alex and he can hammer each other with impunity. As he turns for the clubs, Alex streaks for the small reading group, his arm cocking in his rapid approach, and lands a blow in the middle of Amber's back. As he raises his fist for a second shot he is suddenly in the

170

air on his back in Johnny's arms, legs and arms flailing, and the two disappear into the dark, vacant adjacent room.

"By God that's enough!" Johnny roars as they disappear through the door, and he deposits Alex on the floor; too hard. Alex loses air as his butt hits the hard wood, and in the dimness of the unlighted room there is nothing but Johnny's heaving breathing. Alex glares, astonished, afraid, then full of rage.

He screams, "I hate you!" and Johnny yells back, "I don't care! I'm sick and tired of telling you! Hear me? Sick and tired!"

"I hate you!" Alex screams again, and Johnny grabs his arms, squeezes him. He hates this kid, draws back to slap his face, catches himself, and sees in Alex's flinch everything Johnny has built with him in the past months swirling down the toilet. He releases Alex's arms as if they were electrified, but it's too late, and he moves around behind the bookcase by the door, sitting, listening to his heart pound. On the other side of the bookcase, Alex sniffles, then is quiet.

For an eternity they sit in silence. Johnny breathes deep, tries to relax, but pictures of Edgar flash before him; he sees himself drawing his own five-year-old hand back, slapping Edgar to make him drink. Eyes closed, he touches the floor, almost expecting the texture of the rubber sheet.

"Fuck it for you, Johnny. You did it all wrong." Alex's strong voice breaks the silence.

Johnny has no response, feels the bricks of the walls he has built around his own hideous acts beginning to crumble. He doesn't know what to say. Alex's voice rings in his ears. He's right. Fuck it for me, I did it all wrong.

More silence, then, "Fuck it for you, Johnny. You did it all wrong."

"You gotta quit killin' people in there, Alex."

"I know." His voice says he's sorry.

More silence.

"You did it all wrong."

"I know." Johnny almost whispers it.

And then, as if out of nowhere, Alex is sitting on Johnny's knee, touching his arm. "Let's go back and play."

Johnny considers. "I can't."

"Let's play."

"I'm still too mad, Alex."

"I won't do it no more."

Johnny brings him close, looks into his eyes. Alex speaks the truth; he won't do it no more.

"I know you won't. I'm worried about me."

They sit a while longer. Alex puts his head on Johnny's shoulder.

"How we gonna do this?" Johnny says.

"I won't do it no more," Alex says. "If I get mad, I just hit somethin' that don't be a kid."

It's as simple as that. At least for Alex. They re-enter the room; the aide casts a sideways glance, and Johnny is embarrassed. He and Alex return to the punching bag—Johnny's name now missing from Alex's hit list—the children return from outside, read books, and suddenly it's time to go.

Three times on his way out, Johnny approaches Katherine to tell her what happened, and three times he chickens out. She has such faith in him; he's done so well here. Maybe it was a fluke; it feels under control now. He tells himself he understands it. Alex doesn't rat on him. If it happened again, he'd do it differently.

"But you know different," Wilson says.

"I know different. Wilson, it was my brother's face."

"What's new about that? You see your brother's face every time you lose control."

"This time I saw it while I was going for Alex." Johnny stops, and flood waters gather in his chest. "God, Wilson, I hated my brother. I should have hated my mom, but I hated my brother—because he wouldn't quit peeing his pants. It was like it was his fault I had to hurt him. It was the same with Alex, like he was going to make me hurt him."

A deafening silence, followed by Johnny's gut-wrenching sobs. He feels Wilson's hand between his shoulder blades as his entire body breaks into a sweat. Johnny gasps for air, and finally his breathing slows.

"Johnny," Wilson measures his words. "You didn't kill your brother. Your mother killed your brother. She used you to do it because you were too small and too weak to stop her. You have to get that straight in your head. And in your gut."

"But don't you see? I hated him, Wilson. It felt good to slap him, to make him drink."

"You were five years old, Johnny. It felt like that because of what you believed, not what was true. It was what you believed, and you believed wrong."

"But then I hated Alex . . ."

". . . because . . ."

"Because . . . because . . . because I wanted to get him to stop hurting people, and I couldn't, and I was . . ."

"You were what?"

Johnny's shoulders slump. "I was worthless."

"Just like you were when you were supposed to get your brother to stop peeing."

"Just like." Johnny stops. "So none of this is about Alex. . . ."

"And none of it is about your brother. Who is it about, Johnny? Who is it *always* about?"

Johnny is almost through the waiting room, walking toward the exit, when he turns around, walks slowly back to Wilson's office, hearing Wilson's voice in his head: *Who is it about, Johnny? Who is it always about?*

Wilson looks up from his desk. "What's up?"

"Do you remember saying, 'Tell a little bit of truth, get a little bit of therapy'?"

"Not specifically," Wilson says. "But I say that to everyone."

Johnny takes a deep breath, sits back in his chair. "When I came to you to get me a practicum placement, I told you I took a few years off before college."

Wilson braces. "Yeah."

"I was in jail."

"Violence?"

"I got married."

"They don't usually put you in jail for that." He grimaces, waits.

"We had a baby. A little girl."

Wilson closes his eyes.

"I shook her."

"Oh, man. Is she . . ."

"She's alive," Johnny says, his gaze casting toward his knees, "but she's . . . she'll always be in the institution, never be able to take care of herself. I did two years. I came out, promised myself to make amends."

"So you got your degree and tried to make amends on other people's kids."

It sounds foolish when he hears it out loud. "Yeah."

"God, Johnny, what were you thinking? You could never pass a background check. Even if you get your degree, you'll never . . ." he lets his voice trail off.

"I know."

"And you used me because anyone else would have been more thorough."

"Yeah. I guess. Do you hate me, man?"

Wilson leans back in his chair. "No, Johnny, I don't hate you. I'm just glad nothing happened." He takes another deep breath. "Johnny listen to me. No more secrets. I want you in this office Monday morning. Katherine will be here."

"Oh, no. I couldn't tell her."

"Monday morning," Wilson says. "Be here."

"I'm sorry," Johnny says, seated in his customary chair in Wilson's office the following Monday morning, across the room from Wilson, next to Katherine.

"Tell Alex."

Johnny is quiet, still embarrassed. "I did. And I'm sorry for what I brought into your program."

"Which was . . . ?"

"My meanness," he says. "I should have known I wasn't in control yet."

"You think you couldn't come into my program unless you were in complete control? I'd have to close down if that were the criteria. I'm sure Wilson has said this before, Johnny, but the only way we can deal with our monsters is to bring them out in the open. We have to say their names. It's true for little kids and it's true for us."

Johnny feels frustration, above the always-present rage. He wants to reduce the anxiety, the gnawing. Katherine's right, but words mean nothing here. He just knows he's sorry, and he wants it to be over. God, what an idiot to think he could make up for all he's done; killing his brother, vegetablizing his daughter. Not in this world. Not in this lifetime. Sitting here just brings it back.

Neither Wilson nor Katherine tries to help.

"Look," he says, feeling more heat in his chest and throat. "I messed up, okay? I won't ask you for a letter of recommendation. I'll change my major. I shouldn't have . . ."

Katherine turns to him, puts a hand on his knee like he's seen her do with kids so many times. It brings more anger, being treated like a child. He turns to Wilson. "I shouldn't be . . . I should look for a different line of work, right? I mean, I'm mad just sitting here," and with that the anger drains. *You have to name the monster.*

It's Katherine who answers. "Johnny, you're still one of them. You can't help Alex because you haven't helped the Alex in you yet." She glances over at Wilson. "I just work with kids under five years old. I leave the big kids for the likes of Wilson. Alex isn't hurt; as much as you wanted to do with your anger, you didn't really do much. Only you know how you felt inside, how close you came." She leans closer. "None of this is safe, Johnny. None of it is easy. You can't just decide you're going to make it better without knowing *how,* and you can't make up with the kids at school for what you did in your past. Now I want you to come back out to school and say good-bye the way we planned. You and Wilson will have to figure out the rest."

When Johnny returns to Wilson's office after saying good-bye to the kids at school the following Monday, he runs into a large child's punching bag standing in the middle of the room, the kind that is weighted at the bottom and rights itself after each punch. Painted on the bag is Popeye. Wilson ignores the bag, motions Johnny to his seat.

"So how'd it go? Saying good-bye."

"Okay, I guess. I cried. Couldn't help it."

"That's good," Wilson says. "It's good for kids to see that we have feelings, too."

"I'm going to the registrar this afternoon. Changing my major."

Wilson's eyebrows raise.

"I tried to do it the easy way," Johnny says. "Tried to turn my back on the past."

Wilson smiles. "Yeah, the past has a way of whacking you on the back of the head if you do that."

"That's how I injured my daughter. Thought I could give her a better life than I had just because I wanted to."

Wilson nods to the punching bag. "Remember our friend?"

"Popeye. Yeah, I knocked hell out of him when I used to come here."

"Do you remember his song?"

"Sure," Johnny says, and in his off-key voice sings, "I'm Popeye the Sailor Man, I'm Popeye the Sailor Man. I yam what I yam and that's all what I yam. I'm Popeye the Sailor man."

"I am what I am," Wilson says.

Johnny is quiet, tears welling up.

"You'll know when you 'am' something different," Wilson says. "Meanwhile why don't you take this crusty mariner with you. And set up an appointment with the secretary on your way out."

Johnny picks up the five-foot plastic toy, shakes Wilson's hand, and walks out of the room, humming, "I yam what I yam and that's all what I yam. . . ."

About the Contributors

Laurie Halse Anderson has published several books for younger children and is working on a novel for young adults. Like her protagonist in "Passport," she followed an unconventional path to adulthood. She left home at age sixteen to live on a Danish pig farm. "It wasn't as glamorous as I thought it would be," she admits, "but the people were kind."

Susan Campbell Bartoletti has taught eighth grade for eighteen years while writing fiction and nonfiction for all ages, including *No Man's Land*, a young adult novel. Her *Growing Up in Coal Country* was the recipient of the Carolyn Field Award and the Jane Addams Peace Prize. She got the idea for "Rice Pudding" one day in the car when she realized she and her young teen thought differently about a big issue.

Bruce Coville is the author of some of today's most popular young adult literature, including *My Teacher Is an Alien* and its sequels. About "The Secret of Life According to Aunt Gladys" he says, "I thought it would be interesting to bring a character who had a great deal of emotional energy invested in having a 'normal' family face to face with someone whose very existence challenged that idea in the deepest way possible."

Chris Crutcher won the 1993 ALAN Award for Significant Contribution to the Field of Young Adult Literature, a fitting tribute for an author whose novels have all been named ALA Best Books. He says, " 'Popeye the Sailor' came about because I've worked with so many people who have done astonishing things to children but who aren't really bad people. While there are no excuses for hurting kids, there are almost always reasons, and when we learn those reasons we become a more compassionate society."

Lisa Rowe Fraustino, winner of the PEN Syndicated Fiction Award and the author of *Ash*, an ALA Best Book for Young Adults, teaches "The Modern Young Adult Novel" in the Hollins College graduate program in children's literature. She compiled and edited this anthology after being struck by the idea that censorship begins at home, in the secrets families keep—from the world and from each other.

Anna Grossnickle Hines has written and/or illustrated more than thirty-five books. Today's young adults may remember *Daddy Makes the Best Spaghetti* or *Grandma Gets Grumpy* from their younger years, or perhaps *Boys Are Yucko!* from elementary school. "Stage Fright" is based on her own nauseating valedictory address.

M. E. Kerr was the 1993 recipient of the Margaret A. Edwards Award for significant contribution to the field of Young Adult Literature. Her recent novels, including *Deliver Us from Evie*, continue her tradition of challenging stereotypes and addressing tough themes honestly. When asked how she got the idea for "I Will Not Think of Maine," she replied, "The story just came into my head one day. A revenant at work? Who knows."

Richard Peck won the Edgar Allan Poe Award for *Are You in the House Alone?* as well as the Margaret A. Edwards Award for young adult literature. His most recent young adult novel is *Strays Like Us*. One night in England he looked down from his guest room at the top of Rydal Hall and saw a story in the circle of gravel before the front door. That story became "Waiting for Sebastian."

Dian Curtis Regan is the author of forty books and the recipient of several Children's Choice Awards. In "Words" she wanted to focus on a secret that was unusual and unexpected—yet was just as horrifying upon discovery as abuse or alcoholism.

Graham Salisbury, winner of the 1993 PEN/Norma Klein Award, received the Scott O'Dell Award for *Under the Blood-Red Sun*. Years ago on a beach in Hawaii, where he grew up, he found a water-filled, glass-blown float that Japanese fishermen used to use to hold up nets. He says, "I used to shake it and look into it and dream a zillion wild things. 'Something Like . . . Love' immortalizes that glass ball and all my adolescent dreams."

Rita Williams-Garcia's young adult novels include *Like Sisters on the Homefront*, a Coretta Scott King Honor Book. "About Russell" is based on her own experience growing up with a gifted brother who became lost within himself. She hopes that readers who have experienced the uncertainty and shame of having a loved one with mental illness will feel comforted when they see the disease affects many families.